FLAMINGO LANE

| ALSO BY TIM APPLEGATE |

Fever Tree

FLAMINGO LANE

A NOVEL OF SOUTHERN NOIR

tim applegate

AMBERJACK PUBLISHING
Idaho

Amberjack Publishing
1472 E. Iron Eagle Drive
Eagle, ID 83616
http://amberjackpublishing.com

This book is a work of fiction. Any references to real places are used fictitiously. Names, characters, fictitious places, and events are the products of the author's imagination, and any resemblances to actual persons, living or dead, places, or events is purely coincidental.

Copyright © 2018 by Tim Applegate

Printed in the United States of America. All rights reserved, including the right to reproduce this book, in part or in whole, in any form whatsoever without the prior written permission of the publisher, except in the case of brief quotations embodied in critical reviews and certain other noncommercial uses permitted by copyright law.

Library of Congress Cataloging-in-Publication Data

Names: Applegate, Tim, 1952- author.
Title: Flamingo Lane / by Tim Applegate.
Description: New York : Amberjack Publishing, 2018. | Series: The Yucatan quartet ; 2
Identifiers: LCCN 2018017363 (print) | LCCN 2018017563 (ebook) |
ISBN 9781948705080 (eBook) | ISBN 9781948705073 (pbk. : alk. paper)
Subjects: LCSH: Single women—Fiction. | Kidnapping victims—Fiction. |
Runaways—Fiction. | Drug traffic—Fiction. | GSAFD: Suspense fiction
Classification: LCC PS3601.P66425 (ebook) | LCC PS3601.P66425 F53
2018 (print) | DDC 813/.6—dc23
LC record available at https://lccn.loc.gov/2018017363

For Kerstin and Molly

See the cross-eyed pirates sitting
Perched in the sun
Shooting tin cans
With a sawed-off shotgun.

Bob Dylan, "Farewell Angelina"

Spring, 1982

chance

At sunrise Chance wakes from a night of patchy sleep in a room he doesn't recognize, a room he can't recall. Bare walls, a small window, a pair of cane chairs. Then he remembers the wobbly plane, a two-seater, falling through the clouds before landing on the dusty airstrip, and it all comes rushing back. Yesterday's meeting with Pablo Mestival at the safe house on Isla Mujeres. The return ferry to Cancun over a channel of increasingly bumpy water followed by a drive into the interior with one of Mestival's silent thugs. A clearing in the jungle, streak of grey tarmac, and a single shining plane. Just before they slammed into the kapok trees at the end of the runway, the Cessna lifted up over dense jungle canopy, shuddering in the gusts.

Flexing his stiff back—the mattress he'd slept on was too soft, too mealy—he climbs out of bed and peers out the window, shaking off the cobwebs of sleep. On assignments like this the first few days were always the hardest, and he reminds himself to remain patient, to remain steadfast until the mental fog vanishes and his sense of purpose returns, until he rediscovers the Zen balance, the Zen serenity his dad, that old poseur, instilled in him at the commune in Oregon when he was a boy.

After splashing his face with a trickle of tepid water and yanking a stiff brush through his hair, he strides down a dark hallway into a silent, empty kitchen, where he reaches over the sink, fingers open the blinds, and sees the woman in the backyard hanging clothes on a line. In the distance a red mesa, the sandstone glowing like embers in the morning sun, shadows the desert floor, but the sharp pang in his heart isn't a response to the beauty of that austere landscape, it's a gut reaction to a sudden mental image of his mother, a clothespin clenched in her teeth, lifting one of his shirts to a line.

In retrospect, the commune had been a joke, a tangled path scaling the heights of enlightenment his parents and their friends had so desperately yearned, in vain, to attain. In the end, all that middle-class baggage, all those bourgeois hang-ups they spent years denouncing proved impossible to shed, their unruly cluster of teepees and cabins along a stretch of the Powder River in eastern Oregon nothing more than a pastoral version of the corrupt suburbs in that book of John Cheever's short stories Dieter swapped him in the village in the Yucatan one evening for a chunk of Lebanese hash. Sadly, all those indiscriminate affairs, all those manic episodes of self-medication, all those unpredictable sex and power, sex *as* power undercurrents roiling just beneath the placid surface of Cheever's well-heeled Connecticut neighborhoods was his father's commune all over again.

Carrying her empty laundry basket, the woman slips into the kitchen, regarding Chance with the same indecipherable expression she had worn the night before. A slightly built, taciturn Hispanic in her early forties, she projects the unflinching stoicism the Vietnam vets down in the village in Mexico projected too. No one can touch her. No one can harm her. She's surrounded by a wall.

In the village in the Yucatan those walls—those barricades—came crashing down only when enough tequila had been consumed, enough hashish smoked, enough mescaline chased through the blood with a swallow of cold *cerveza*. Then the bonfire would be lit, the bottle passed, a guitar softly strummed. For a time, bonds that felt as unbreakable as iron were forged in the fire of that chemical high, the hippies and poets, veterans and draft dodgers, runaways and strays temporary replacements for the families they had all left behind. True companions. *Compañeros*. Someone would recognize the song the guitarist was playing—Neil Young's "Helpless" or Joni Mitchell's "Clouds"—and sing the chorus. Then the others would join in.

And yet all the while it was the Vietnam vets, Bobby Parrish and his brothers-in-arms, who understood that these moments of happiness, like all moments of happiness, were transitory. Even on a tropical beach. Especially on a tropical beach.

The woman indicates the coffeepot on the counter and Chance nods, determined to match her reticence with his own. Every day was a war of wills. But he was used to that.

He's waiting for the man from town, the one who picked him up at the airstrip the previous evening, to deliver the car. Which might take a day. Or a week. At this point his schedule, his itinerary, is in the hands of someone else, and that's why he's so frustrated. The plan's in place and he's ready to get on with it. Of course he could always ask the woman when the driver's coming back, but even if she knows, which isn't likely, she probably won't tell him.

Without a word she places a chunk of stale coffee cake on a chipped white plate on the table next to his cup. Then, cradling a second basket of laundry, she steps back outside. Chewing the rubbery cake, Chance tracks her as she crosses the yard and begins to pin more garments to the line, including a pair of flimsy white panties that immediately generates, despite his resolve to stay focused, to keep his eyes on the prize, a pulse of heat. But he won't think about that now. As part of the purification, he won't think about that now. He takes a gulp of lukewarm coffee to wash down the tasteless cake and slides the plate away, no longer hungry. Meanwhile, out the window, in the shadow of the mesa, the woman turns her back to him and bends lithely down to pick up the empty basket, and Chance wonders if she knows that he's staring at her, if that's why she bent over that way.

At the commune in Oregon, the wash line had been strung between two cottonwoods perched on a flat rectangle of grass above the banks of the Powder River. Once a week his mother and her friends hung their clothes there, a colorful tapestry of tie-dyed T-shirts, frilly summer dresses, patched-at-the-knee jeans. Pinning the clothes to the line, the women would laugh, whisper, and glance back toward the fire pit to make sure that none of the men who had gathered around the embers to ward off the morning chill were eavesdropping. Only Chance, quiet and watchful and too young to pose a threat, was allowed to hear what they had to say, was allowed to share their feminine secrets.

In Cheever's short stories errant husbands stole illicit kisses behind closed doors, but Chance's father was more careless than that. One morning as the boy trotted back from a solitary run along the river he spied his dad and a woman who called herself Peony standing in the shadows of the communal dining hall, talking. That's all they appeared to be doing, chatting, but something about their gestures—Chance's father leaning down toward the woman in confidence, Peony unconsciously touching his sleeve—caused the boy to suspect that there was more going on than idle conversation.

In the following days he covertly stalked his father, his first taste of surveillance, as he went about his duties as one of the commune's leaders—checking the food stocks, supervising the construction of a new sauna, listening to complaints—and what the boy eventually discovered crushed him. Instead of stealing kisses behind a bedroom door, Chance's dad stole his, and more, anywhere and everywhere he could: inside the smokehouse, on the steep trail up the spine of the mountain, in one of the teepees recently abandoned by a family disillusioned not with the ideals of the tribe but by its behavior, which, like his father's, betrayed those ideals.

And that wasn't all. If Chance thought (or more accurately, hoped) that Peony was the sole object of his father's affections, he soon discovered the ugly truth. Like one of Cheever's fallen heroes, his father didn't discriminate in the matter of partners. As far as the boy could determine, practically every woman in the commune, married or not, had at one time or another been the target of his advances. And more than a few had succumbed.

The boy brooded. His mother represented, as always, the center of his universe, the sun he depended on for sustenance and warmth. And even though the father had been there too, from the beginning, it wasn't the same. If the mother was the sun the boy-planet revolved around, the father was the moon, cold and distant, spectral. It wasn't that he ignored the boy, far from it. On various occasions he showed him how to fly-fish for trout, chop firewood without slicing off a toe, or prime a faulty pump, skills that would serve him well later on. But he did so without affection or love, less a doting father than a master craftsman helping a wide-eyed apprentice learn a useful trade. And now he had taught his son something else, something obscene. Marital vows meant nothing, trust was an illusion, fidelity a lie. Time and again the boy covertly witnessed his father's seductions, and soon his youthful brooding gave way to rage.

In the bedroom of the safe house, he hears a car pull into the drive and reminds himself once again that patience is the key. Glancing out the window, he inhales a few sharp breaths—*pranayama*—while the man who escorted him to the safe house the night before slides out of a dark blue Monte Carlo and marches toward the front door, jingling a set of keys.

Even though the sun is already slipping behind the western hills, their contours in the falling light as soft as loaves of bread, Chance considers leaving that evening instead of the following day. He could drive all night, make Santa Fe by sunup, then crash for a while at a rest stop before the heat sets in. But then again, why rush it? As far as he knows, his target isn't going anywhere, so why the hurry? What's one more day? Instead of a rash, impulsive gesture, it would be better, he finally decides, to get a fresh start in the morning after a good night's sleep.

To Chance's surprise the woman sits directly across the table that night, watching him demolish her chorizo tacos, avocado salad, bowl of pinto beans flecked with slivers of ham. Halfway through the meal she stands up and goes over to the fridge and brings back a second bottle of *cerveza*, and even though he knows that she's only doing what Pablo Mestival pays her to do, feeding and housing one of his contractors, she seems slightly less guarded now, fractionally more relaxed. He spoons up the last of the pinto beans then tilts the second bottle and finishes that off too. But when the woman starts to rise again, presumably to bring him another *cerveza*, he reaches out, not quite touching her, and shakes his head.

No more, *por favor*. *Gracias*. Then he catches the woman's eye and for once, she doesn't turn away.

Habla Inglés?

She appears reluctant to answer but eventually relents, spreading a thumb and a finger an inch apart.

A little?

Sí, she answers, a leetle.

He asks her if she's married and she replies no more.

No more?

My husband, she says without emotion, ees dead.

Chance glances out the window, imagining years here, in this barren desert, all alone. I'm sorry, he says.

Her response, her pinched smile, is impossible to decipher. Bitterness? Sarcasm? Fear? She swivels around on her chair and points out the window. There, she murmurs. Right there.

Chance points too.

He died out there? In the yard?

Not died, keeled. The woman lifts a hand, pretending to clutch a pistol, pretending to squeeze off a shot. Right by, how you say? With her small fingers she mimics pinning clothes.

The clothesline?

Sí, he was killed out there. By the clothesline.

Instead of imagining the scene—the husband bleeding out beneath her blouses—Chance once again sees the woman bend over the laundry basket to attract him. Or not. She knew he had been watching her when she leaned over. Or he hadn't, at that moment, crossed her mind. If he made a move toward her this evening, she would accept his advances. Or plunge a knife into his heart.

At the sink, she washes and rinses his dishes, her movements quick and decisive now, almost fierce. She looks upset, perhaps ashamed to have mentioned her husband in front of a stranger. Sliding a plate into a slot in the strainer, she turns back to him, and once again her expression remains unreadable. Chance recalls the psychological term for it: *flat affect*, the inability to express emotion.

You will be leaving soon?

In the morning, he replies. He stands up and grabs the two empty beer bottles and places them on the counter. Early, he adds, though the woman, furiously wiping her hands on a dish towel, no longer seems aware that he's even there, in her kitchen, gazing out the window at the dusty ground beneath the clothesline where her husband died.

The next morning he wakes at sunrise again, at the first rumor of light, remembering how his father had been an early riser too, often rising before dawn. Sometimes Chance would hear the cabin door close and he would finger open the curtains next to his bed and watch his father carry his yoga mat to the bank above the Powder River, where he would stretch the kinks out of his lanky frame by assuming his favorite positions: The Bridge, The Extended Triangle, The Mountain Pose.

The last time Chance saw him—in hospital, a few days before he died—he had tried to conjure up some kind of tangible feeling, pity or sadness or regret, but failed to do so. Why lie, especially to yourself?

The old poseur had suffered an aneurysm and lay unconscious on the bed. Chance stared at the haggard face, which was strangely calm, perhaps accepting, at last, his inevitable demise. At some point a nurse entered the room and checked his father's pulse and smiled sympathetically at the son, but none of it meant a thing. You live and you die, he thought. You harm some and help others but mostly you tend to yourself. It was that simple. Absurdly, on his way out the door, he had wheeled around, winked at the man in the coma, and given him a mock salute.

Now in the safe house, in the first flush of dawn, he zips up the duffel, tosses a couple of wrinkled dollar bills on the bed, and re-checks the side pocket of his valise to make sure he hasn't forgotten the file on Faye Lindstrom, the woman they used to call Angelina when they were all young and happy and living on borrowed time in a village in Quintana Roo.

faye

No, it was unacceptable, untenable, absurd. Her mother's false cheer. Her father's clumsy attempts at idle conversation over a bowl of beef stew. The disastrous trip to Baesler's Market the afternoon she ran into her former schoolmate, Cathy what's her name, who, clueless, wanted to know what Faye *had been up to all these years.* No, it was impossible, intolerable, she had to get away.

And yet the old neighborhood at dusk—all those familiar two-story houses on South Tenth Street—still tugs at her heart when she sits alone out on the porch swing after dinner, a cool breeze wafting through the black screens and the stars blinking on over the sycamore. On certain nights she hears the faint whistle of a freight train cutting through a distant field and her childhood comes flooding back, a swollen river cresting its narrow banks as she recalls how she used to lie in her bed or lounge on this porch swing listening to the trains and dreaming of all the exotic places she would one day visit. Places like Quintana Roo.

But that has all changed. She spent four years in exotic places all right—in the village on the sea then in safe houses scattered across the Yucatan—and she has come home damaged, possibly beyond repair.

The garish aisles at Baesler's Market could have been a set on a TV show, the cases of Heineken too green, the boxes of Wheaties too boxy, the muzak pumped out over the loudspeakers too loud. If only the world would calm down. Why did everyone have to pretend to be so happy?

Trying to keep up with her mother as she raced through the produce section, Faye suppressed the sudden aching urge for a shot of smack to calm her nerves by silently repeating the promise she had made to herself a thousand times during the nightmarish two weeks she had recently spent in detox: now that she was finally clean, she would never touch a needle again.

As brisk and efficient as a Stepford Wife, Blanche Lindstrom marched up and down the bright aisles, tossing a box of mac and cheese or a plastic jar of apple sauce into her cart without breaking stride. To Faye's amazement her mother didn't even consult a list, opting instead to purchase her groceries in a burst of spontaneity that seemed to the bewildered daughter one step away from hysteria. The term was impulse shopping, but it looked a bit more desperate than that.

Ever since the private detective her parents had hired brought her home from Mexico, her mother had shifted into overdrive, presuming, Faye supposed, that the best way to ward off the evil spirits that must surely still inhabit her daughter's haunted soul was by drowning them in an ocean of goodwill. No string of garlic bulbs or silver dagger to the heart for Blanche Lindstrom; to defeat the forces of darkness, her mother was determined to put her brave face on, projecting fey, girlish gaiety at every opportunity, as if to convince Faye that she was out of harm's way now even though she must have known that no one who had suffered what her daughter had suffered would fall for such a ruse.

It'll do you good, Blanche had cheerfully suggested. We'll get some fresh air. Buy a couple sundaes at Dairy Queen. Swing by Baesler's and pick up some food.

It had sounded like a terrible idea. Why did she have to leave the comfort, the shelter, the safety of her childhood home?

Faye? Faye Lindstrom?

Startled, Faye spun around as a young woman wheeling a shopping cart past a kosher pickle display stopped dead in her tracks. Faye Lindstrom? Is that you?

Excuse me?

Cathy, the woman exclaimed, pointing at her chest. It's Cathy!

In retrospect, Faye must have realized that sooner or later she was bound to encounter someone from her past—Terre Haute was, after all, her hometown—yet she remained ill-prepared.

It's Cathy, silly! Cathy Mapes!

The woman's face was a sepia-tinged snapshot from some distant, forgotten past. In a daze, in a dream, Faye accepted Cathy's hand and even managed to squeeze out a strained smile. But when her former schoolmate demanded to know what she had been up to all these years, all she could do was shrug her shoulders and murmur something noncommittal—*oh you know, this and that*—until her mother cut in and saved the day by asking Cathy about her parents. Keeping her eyes on Faye, Cathy told Blanche that her parents were just fine.

Based on the look on her schoolmate's face, *this and that* must have stung, must have sounded both evasive and rude. But what other choice did she have? Well let's see, Cath, first I left town to live with a bunch of hippies in a village in Mexico. Then I fell in love with a brutal drug lord who turned me into a junkie and a sexual slave. So how *you* been?

No, it was unacceptable, indefensible, she had to get away. She was grateful to her parents for their unconditional support, no matter how ineffectual that support might be, but she couldn't shake the feeling that she was nothing more than a captive again, trapped in her childhood home this time, afraid to venture out lest she run into another old acquaintance. Sleeping late, eating desultory meals, reading overwritten novels with too many narrative threads to keep track of, she wasted her days. And the nights were no better. Still awake at four a.m., the hour of doom, she padded over to the bedroom window and peered down at the sidewalk, certain that one of Mestival's henchmen would be out there waiting, in the windy shadows of the sycamore, to drag her back to Quintana Roo.

Her father brooded over his bowl of beef stew, listlessly stabbing at a carrot swimming in the murky broth. Then he lifted his head and looked across the table with an abrupt, enigmatic grin, as if he had just remembered something that might sweep away the black cloud that had been hanging over the house ever since Faye came home.

So I ran into Bill Simpson this morning down at the bank. You remember Bill?

Faye recalled a boy with beady eyes and a shock of unruly red hair. She tentatively nodded.

Well he owns a sporting goods store now, over on Poplar.

The one his uncle owned, Faye said.

That's right, the one his uncle owned.

In Faye's eyes, her father, once so steadfast, looked a little crazed, Blanche's double.

Anyway, he asked about you. Ain't that something? And he mentioned a job opening.

Just like that.

Just like that!

Blanche put down her spoon, predictably beaming. What kinda job, honey?

Oh you know, sales. Clerking.

And he mentioned me, Faye said.

He mentioned you! Said he remembered what a fine athlete you were in school, all those sports you played. Said you'd be a natural.

A natural?

For the job.

Pushing her bowl away, Faye looked across the table at her parents with a twinge of guilt. All they wanted, she knew, was for their prodigal daughter to rediscover, in the darkness of her despair, some glimmer of hope, some glimmer of happiness. But how could they possibly understand how she (or Bobby Parrish or the other Vietnam vets in the village, or anyone else for that matter, who had ever been physically or emotionally traumatized) felt? How could they possibly imagine what she had been through?

One night on the beach Parrish had plopped down next to her clutching a bottle of mescal. In the unsteady glow of the bonfire he looked craven, feral. Ya can't ya know, he slurred.

He looked feral and yet Faye, like the rest of them, had known only his kindness, his gentle regard.

Can't?

Go home again.

His beard, she noticed as he leaned in close, was a few days old, black stubble. Because home is still home, he whispered, *but you*—a long pause—*are no longer you.*

Stuttering an apology for barely touching her beef stew, Faye excused herself from the table and fled. Upstairs she lay face down on her bed, inconsolable. Then she heard the wind in the tree and went over to the window to watch the boughs of the sycamore clatter and sway. When she was a girl she had cherished this view: towering tree, patch of green lawn, telephone wire humming with the voices of her neighbors. Sometimes a hawk would soar down and perch on the wire and Faye would tremble at the wonder of it all, the world's exquisite components matching, in tenderness, in beauty, her enchanted life.

Only her sister Hannah understands her dilemma, her frustration, her indescribable fear. But Hannah has her own life to live and it isn't fair to expect her to race over to the house every ten minutes to help her sister cope. No, the only viable option is to leave, to pack her bags and hole up some place where no one knows who she is. Catch a Greyhound to Wichita or Baltimore or Portland, Maine. Rent a room in a boarding house and lose herself in the cacophony, the mad swirl, the anonymity of the streets.

Howie Goodman.

Who?

Howie Goodman. Remember Howie? From grade school? He owns one of those fancy new yogurt shops now.

And he mentioned me.

He mentioned you! Ain't that something?

That's something.

Didn't you guys date once?

I don't remember, Dad.

Anyway, he asked if he could stop by some day. You know, to catch up.

Finally one rainy, desolate Sunday morning, crawling out of her skin with anxiety, Faye picks up the phone and dials Dieter.

chance

In the blue Monte Carlo he cruises north then west then north again, pedal to the metal on a nearly deserted state highway where the aspens are beginning to leaf and chili peppers dangle from the front-porch rafters of an occasional adobe home. Then back down to the speed limit, shifting into cruise control as he ramps onto I-25 east of Santa Fe. Because he can't afford to be stopped. As far as he knows his papers are in order, the registration on the Monte Carlo clean, but still, even a minor traffic infraction might raise a red flag somewhere. He glances down at the speedometer and lifts his foot off the gas, reminding himself once again to remain patient. Patience, determination, resolve: his Shaolin principles, his Bodhisattva guideposts, his Tao.

On the radio he discovers an alternative station out of Albuquerque featuring a suite of songs by Cream back in the days when the mods and rockers spray painted on the bleak grey walls of London *Clapton is God*, that soaring, legendary guitar a perfect match for his decidedly chipper mood this morning following a sound night's sleep undisturbed by dreams or insomnia.

In Eugene, during his one semester of college, Cream was the kind of band that put his girlfriend Mindy in the mood, not that she needed much to reach that exalted state. Clapton, The Doors, Santana—a few expert guitar licks, along with a toke or two of his friend Stick's seemingly endless supply of Acapulco Gold, was all it usually took. To ease the sexual tension, Mindy's roommate Beth would glide past them out the door, grinning, so they could do it in peace. The sun streaming through Mindy's bedroom window glowed on their heated skin, their feverish gyrations. In the background, those phallic guitars rising in crescendo lifted them too, and when Chance squeezed his eyes shut a thousand suns burst into flames. But then sadly, inevitably, the little death downer immediately afterwards, the random lines of a poem he read once burning its viral message into his mind: *If she comes so easily / what must she be to other men*?

After a quick lunch, a Caesar salad at a roadside diner, he checks his wristwatch: a few minutes past one. At this rate he should reach Denver by dusk. Drink a couple beers. Grab a bite to eat. Settle in for the evening at a decent motel where, with any luck, he won't dream, as he does so often, about Mindy. Or Faye.

North then east then north again, still locked into that rhythm, into that sturdy old rock-and-roll vibe. He twists the dial to raise the volume on the opening chords of Dylan's "Positively Fourth Street," recalling how a blur of static on a portable radio on a Yucatan beach the night he tried to seduce Faye Lindstrom suddenly cleared, giving way, faintly at first then in full sonic mode, to another one of the songwriter's familiar titles: fittingly, on that desolate evening, "Desolation Row." What were the odds that one of the rock icon's anthems—not even one of his hits—would provide the somber background music for the abrupt dissolution of his relationship with a woman so infatuated with Dylan she nicknamed herself after one of his songs?

When the static cleared and "Desolation Row" came on, Angelina had abruptly stood up, shaking her head and brushing the sand from her dress. Swaying like the trunk of a slender palm in the Yucatan breeze, she apologized, profusely. She just didn't think of him that way, she said. Their relationship was deeper than that.

He had risen from the sand too, awkwardly, achingly tumescent. Deeper?

Our friendship, she cried. It's much more important than—she swept a pale hand through the air, as if to scatter the seeds of his misplaced lust—than all this.

Chance had clenched his fists, seething. Sometimes the wholesome, nurturing, mother earth persona Angelina projected fit her to a T. And yet he knew, everyone knew, that on certain nights she slipped into some lucky expat's bed—usually one of the soldiers—to offer him the solace she now so resolutely withheld. He turned away to stare out to sea, helpless, powerless, for the second time in two years wounded to the core by someone he loved.

He drives steadily, effortlessly, crossing into southern Colorado while remaining in cruise control even as he whips past a station wagon struggling up one of the steep mountain grades. He's always been fond of road trips, but his recollection of that night on the beach has darkened his mood and stained his psyche, and it's hard for him to appreciate the stark beauty of the vistas flowing by. Still, you had to accept these debilitating emotional episodes, these crushing memories, if you were going to survive. He had learned long ago that if you wanted to maintain your balance and remain on an even keel—and what better described a Shaolin?—there were going to be times when you had to embrace your own agony. You could lie in bed in a dark room and chug a fifth of cheap booze, or you could rise above the torment and clinically examine, instead, the roots of your despair. Examine. Dissect. And eventually, destroy.

One afternoon in Eugene, Mindy's roommate Beth, visibly conflicted about what she was about to do, met him in a city park. Where, on a wooden bench facing the Willamette River, she spit out the brutal truth. His girlfriend, his beloved, was promiscuous, shockingly promiscuous, with other men. With lots of other men.

Stunned, he watched autumn leaves ride the current downstream, two or three swallows loop from tree to tree at river's edge. It was a beautiful spot, a Saturday afternoon picnic spot, and yet that day it had seemed as barren as the surface of the moon. He demanded to know who.

Beth stared down at the ground, almost as miserable as he was. Tommy, she murmured.

Chance couldn't believe his ears. Tommy? She's been banging Tommy?

Frank.

He wanted to grab something, to smash something to pieces with his hands.

Frank?

Beth's voice was a drill in his ear, chalk on a blackboard. Pablo, she insisted. Stick. Joe.

It was more than he could bear. He tried to tune out Beth's words by concentrating on the river, on the swallows in the trees, on the autumn sky so heartbreakingly blue that day, but at that moment Beth reached out and touched his cheek, gently turning him towards her.

Don't you see, sweetie? She fucks pretty much anyone, pretty much everyone. How could you not know? Everyone knows!

Kissing Beth on the cheek to acknowledge her kindness (for that is what her gesture, despite the pain it caused, ultimately represented, a kindness), he walked back along the river to his apartment. Like boulders tumbling down a hillside, Beth's startling revelations had shattered the glass walls of his denial. And yet somehow those same poisonous revelations had also given him a glimpse of a life unbound by the chains of what society, what the bourgeois, considered proper. Existentially he was free to do whatever he wanted to do, and for the first time, when he contemplated what it might feel like to end someone's life, it struck him as a viable option.

Now as he negotiates his way between a pickup in the passing lane and a cherry-red Mustang on the right, he catches a glimpse of his reflection in the rear-view mirror. Sun-bleached blond hair cut long and parted in the middle, surfer style. Wraparound shades concealing pale blue eyes and crow's feet too, first wrinkles deepened by all those days in the tropical sun. Strong jaw and thin lips breaking into a smile as he considers how, in a few days, vengeance will be his.

dieter

Maggie pauses in the kitchen doorway, looking out at the flagstone patio where Dieter is busy composing notes—seeds, at this point, scattered across a barren field. She's clutching a cordless phone.

It's for you.

He looks up with a pinch of irritation. The novel he's working on, the sequel to *Fever Tree*, has run into a roadblock and now, to double his frustration, his wife disrupts his train of thought. Has he not asked her a thousand times not to interrupt him when he's working?

Tell him I'll call back.

Maggie shakes her head, irritated now too. She's told him before: I'm not your secretary, I'm your wife.

It's a her, she says without inflection.

What?

It's not a him, it's a her.

Fine. Tell *her* I'll call back.

No. Maggie marches across the flagstones and hands him the phone. *You* tell her.

He follows his usual route to the harbor, passing through the genteel neighborhood where he lives—most of the houses antebellum and doggedly well-kept—into the town square, an X of sidewalks crisscrossing the center of the plaza like the axis of a wheel. On the park benches scattered around the four spokes of that wheel a few shoppers have stopped to rest, scanning the local paper or folding the sports section into a fan.

He waits for the red light to change then crosses Main Street, flashing back to the day four years before when he pulled into Crooked River a few weeks after his wife Jen was killed by a drunk driver on a rainy highway in southern Indiana. He was deep in the fog of grief at the time, but he still remembers his first sight of this now-familiar central square where, he would later write, *a number of buildings stood empty, For Sale or Lease signs taped to their dusty windows though there were a few encouraging glimmers of hope too, stubborn businesses that had found a way, in the face of falling profits, to hang on.* And now four years later many of those landmark businesses—the Gibson Hotel, Patterson's Antiques, Keller's Hardware—remain open. Including, perhaps most surprisingly of all, Nirvana, the hippie emporium where *those who had strayed off the path of righteousness could purchase a Jimi Hendrix headband, the latest album by Led Zeppelin, or a hookah from Katmandu.*

As he approaches the marina, a shrimp trawler wobbles back to its berth, a dripping net draped over the skimmer frame and red and yellow buoys lashed to its weathered wooden hull. Spotting the writer, one of the deckhands raises a hand and calls out his name and Dieter waves back in reply, pleased by the recognition. Most of the local fishermen have never read his books but they've heard that the harbor in Crooked River was prominently featured in the last one and that the portrait of deckhands and ship captains and the difficult work they perform was respectful. And of course, like everyone else in town, they secretly hope (or in some rare cases fear) that the writer will include them in his next novel.

At The Tides, a popular, often raucous tavern at the far end of the docks, he opts to sit outside at a quiet table facing the harbor. Placing a pint of Bass ale next to his notebook, he takes out his pen. Fortunately the locals gathered inside at the bar know not to disturb him when he's working, know not to stop and chat when they see him scribbling notes in his journal or mumbling lines of dialogue to himself. He's a writer, after all, and they've discovered that writers, if Dieter is any indication, guard these moments of privacy the way a rich man guards his cache of gold. Besides, as a regular at The Tides his is a familiar and predictable M.O. After going over the notes and finishing his first ale, he'll belly up to the bar and order a second pint and join in the general conversation. Ever curious, he'll ask them about the quality of the fishing these days, the rumors of a spring storm racing up the Gulf, or the early-season baseball scores.

As he flips open his journal he notices out of the corner of his eye the *Patti Belle*, a single-mast Bermuda sloop often seen in moorage at the marina, sailing out to sea. On the deck, a thirtyish woman in a red halter top and cutoff jeans adjusts the boat's starboard tack until the mainsail bulges and the sloop reaches speed. Tracking the boat's progress he wonders, not for the first time, if the woman behind the wheel is indeed Patti Belle, if one day in a burst of immodesty she purchased a can of red paint and a tapered marine brush from Keller's Hardware and christened the sloop with her own name. Which, now that he thinks about it, would be fitting. For even though a companion occasionally tags along, Patti usually sails alone.

He tries to refocus on his notes but has trouble concentrating because he's still out of synch, still distracted by the phone call from Faye Lindstrom. Unsurprisingly—they hadn't spoken in four years—she had sounded nervous. And even though he was nervous too, he had replied that he was glad to hear from her (he was), that of course he wanted to see her (he did), and that yes, next week would be fine. And yet throughout the course of their conversation he was aware, in the back of his mind, of a tremor of doubt, a tremor of trepidation.

Watching the *Patti Belle* glide past the rock jetty at the northern end of the harbor, he recalls the Faye, the Angelina, he knew back in Quintana Roo. Flower child with sparkling blue eyes and a cascade of straight brown hair held in place by a red and white headband, earth mother with an open, guileless smile, trusted friend it was impossible not to feel a spiritual connection with, Angelina, like his first wife Jen, represented an ideal that seemed to Dieter, in retrospect, as quaint as love beads. For while the others paid verbal homage to their fashionable beliefs (peace and love, world harmony, spiritual balance) Angelina lived by those beliefs. When a member of the tribe drank too much mescal or smoked one too many Thai sticks and began to rave about his parents, who didn't understand him, or his government, which had sent him over to a godforsaken country to die for no reason at all, it was Angelina who clutched the man's hand, walked him back to his cabana, and listened to his sad revelations. With the soldiers she was especially gentle, sometimes sleeping with one of them not only to satisfy his, and her, lust, but also out of a pool of compassion that seemed bottomless. In the middle of the night, when they moaned and thrashed in the fever grip of some terrifying dream, she rubbed their tense shoulders with patchouli oil or traced the scars of shrapnel down the length of their sinewy arms to lull them back to sleep.

And then one day Pablo Mestival showed up, and before any of the expats could fathom what was happening, Angelina, like the *Patti Belle*, sailed away.

In his cups, Dieter hovers over the adobe grill, silver tongs gleaming in the shadows or slashing through the plumes of white smoke that lift from the embers and curl sideways in the breeze. In the pool, Hunter dives for the quarter he just tossed into the deep end while a few feet away Sunny, their yellow Labrador, sleeps beneath lemons that hang, like Christmas baubles, from a puzzle of spindly boughs.

Squinting at the smoke and nursing a ruby-red glass of Cabernet, Dieter looms over the grill in his usual khaki shorts, Indiana University T-shirt, and well-worn flip flops, his pageboy haircut framing a thin, boyish face that Maggie fears one day soon will start to look gaunt. Thirty-two next month he has not, like some men his age, developed a premature paunch or begun to lose his hair. But still, time takes its toll on boyish faces too, just as it does on writers, especially, she assumes, on writers like Dieter who drink.

He clutches the silver tongs, patiently monitoring the three rib-eyes in the center of a circle of Anaheim peppers cored and seeded then filled with a rich herbed cream cheese that has Maggie counting calories, though she really needn't worry: for the last few years the scales have held steady at 140 pounds, more or less the same weight she carried in college. In *Fever Tree* Dieter compared her to a young Colleen Dewhurst but Maggie thought Maureen O'Hara would have been more apt. Because Maggie knows exactly what draws men to her, which is not what her father used to refer to as her southern sass. Early on she discovered that men were visual creatures—a glimpse of a pretty girl in a skimpy bikini pretty much kneecapped them for the rest of the day—and naturally concluded that what attracted them wasn't her sass or intelligence or her syrupy southern charm, attributes she possessed in spades. What attracted them was that Maureen O'Hara-like flame of red hair crowning a glimpse of bare shoulders and an ample curve of breast.

Not that she dotes on such matters anymore, or at least not as much as she used to. Three years married to an acclaimed writer with a steady, if not spectacular, income, she owns a restored antebellum house in her beloved hometown as well as a rustic summer home on two woodsy acres in southern Indiana. She's raising a handsome, and surprisingly well-behaved, teenaged son. Now that she no longer has to work for a wage, she spends much of her free time volunteering for Crooked River's Garden Club, the local Audubon Society, and Bloomington's Meals on Wheels. And when she adds all this up she understands the envy of so many of her friends, as well as her sister Lureen. So why, lately, has she been feeling so dissatisfied? And why, lately, has she found herself not only noticing the wayward glances of men on the street but locking into their hungry eyes, which are often as boldly sexual as a hand slipping underneath the hem of her skirt? Has the fact that for the last year or so her orgasms—when, that is, she has had one—have been tame and mechanical, almost *contemplative* versions of the tumbling-over-the-waterfall-and-landing-with-a-mighty-splash-in-a-pool-of-warm-water kind she used to have, clouded her judgment? And has she become so shallow, so primal that she now considers her husband's most important function not the novels he's writing for posterity but his ability to perform like a porn star in bed?

On more than one occasion she considered diplomatically mentioning her dilemma to Dieter then quickly dismissed the idea. First, his not inconsiderable but nonetheless fragile ego would be pierced and deflated. And second, when you were married to a novelist you never knew if, or how, you might be portrayed in his next book. Writers placed their work above every other concern, and sometimes she wonders how many men and women remained with their writer-spouses merely because they were afraid that if they fled, those spouses, like Philip Roth, might skewer them in a *roman à clef.*

No longer concerned with calories, she polishes off the last Anaheim pepper, swallows a gulp of Cabernet, and sets her fork down on the plate next to a withered strip of gristle, which is all that's left of her steak.

So this woman who called, Faye. She's the one you told me about, right?

Right.

The one you're writing about.

Yeah, the one I'm writing about.

Maggie swirls what's left of the wine in her glass, a small, sloshy red wave. The one who was held captive, she sighs. The one you all thought was dead.

Yeah, that one. Angelina.

Wait a minute, I thought her name was Faye.

It is. But down there it was Angelina. After the Dylan song.

Maggie looks over at Sunny lying with crossed paws at the edge of the flagstones, waiting for one of them to toss her a scrap. *Down there*, she muses. How many times has she heard him use that phrase? It was practically his mantra.

And she wants to see you now. After all this time, she wants to see you.

Dieter shrugs, swirling his wine too.

You know you sound kinda funny about this.

Funny?

Skeptical.

Unbidden, a picture of her tumbling over that waterfall in the arms of another man—no one in particular, just any other man—whirls through her mind and she stutters No, no, I was just wondering, you know . . .

If she's stable?

Yeah, if she's stable. I mean she's gonna be watching the house, right? Watching Sunny?

Dieter pauses, choosing his words. Look, I know this is awful sudden, this whole idea. But why not? Lureen could watch the dog but having someone here might be better. Angeli . . . Faye can take him out for walks, take him to the beach. It's a lot to ask your sister every summer. You said so yourself.

Maggie looks blearily up at the sky. So many stars. So much distance. What was really out there? Her born-again sister opted for the easy answer, Heaven or Hell, but Maggie, a skeptic at heart, doesn't have that luxury.

But she'll be all alone, she murmurs.

And that's what she wants, Dieter assures her. Solitude. Anonymity.

Maggie can remember when all *she* wanted was her husband and son, when she considered a woman canning tomatoes in a country kitchen in Indiana while her son raked leaves and her husband finished another chapter in his new novel a perfect morning. Now she isn't so sure. Of anything.

Fine. I'll leave her Lureen's number. In case she needs anything.

Good idea . . . I suppose.

Maggie shoots him a look. She doesn't trust that mischievous grin.

You suppose?

Yeah, I suppose. That it's a good idea. As long as Lureen doesn't, you know, try to convert her.

Dieter . . . she warns.

Or try to get her laid.

Dieter!

I'm just sayin'.

You're just sayin' what?

chance

As the sun lifted over the foothills into a dome of blue sky, he checked out of his motel room, shifted the Monte Carlo into cruise control, and dropped down from the mountains into the high-prairie plains of the great western nowhere.

Limon, Flagler, Stratton. Flat, windy towns with redbrick storefronts, rows of battered pickups parked at angles along Main Street, men in camo sitting down at the counter of the local diner to plates of steaks and eggs.

Emerald wheat fields, newly planted, burnished by the sun. Freight cars abandoned on weedy spurs that haven't been active for years. Water towers spray painted with cryptic symbols by some local teenaged scribe.

Midmorning he pulled into a rest stop just over the Kansas state line. Carrying his yoga mat, he chose a patch of sparse grass next to the restrooms to assume his various poses—The Dolphin, Dragonfly, Down Dog Split—until the cramped muscles in his arms and shoulders stretched, loosened, and relaxed. Tension free, he performed a few minutes of *pranayama*, each deep, purifying breath a reaffirmation of spiritual health, spiritual cleansing. In a state of serenity, he pictured a swift river plunging through a sandstone canyon circled by the spirit bird that protects errant pilgrims from harm.

Then he opened his eyes and saw a truck driver stomp past with a pronounced scowl for the surfer boy sitting cross-legged on some kind of rubber mat pretending to be Buddha. Grinning, he offered the trucker a thumbs-up.

One day, he vowed, he would pen his memoirs, record his remarkable journey for posterity's sake. Technically, of course, he isn't a writer—he has never even kept a diary—but he could always attend some classes or call his friend Dieter for advice. Because the world needed this book, he decided, the way it had needed Ginsberg's *Howl* or Kerouac's *On the Road*, kindred accounts of the rejection of societal values (in his case, bogus hippie values) in favor of spiritual bliss.

Yes, he could see it now, the accolades in Newsweek, the congratulatory letter from Dieter, the rapt faces of his fans gazing up at the stage where their beloved author, reading glasses perched on the tip of his nose, described his picaresque adventures.

Fortunately, over the years, he has meticulously kept and filed all the snapshots taken from Powder River on, photographic evidence that will silence any naysayers who might choose to doubt the veracity of his outrageous claims.

The first one was a Canon 7 his dad gave him when they were living at the commune on the Powder River, a compact camera that fit easily inside his hand. Later, poring over manuals, he mastered the complex language of advanced photography: lens and filter, light meter and shutter speed, focusing screens. And yet on this particular assignment a simple point-and-shoot Minolta is all he carries, all he needs. The composition not the technology, the eye not the science is what really mattered. The eye and the Shaolin concentration. The task at hand.

Colby. Oakley. Grainfield. If he were recording this assignment, he would shoot Kansas in black and white, like the movie versions of *Paper Moon* and *In Cold Blood* he watched with Dieter in his room above the dive shop in Quintana Roo.

Kansas. Roads straight as switchblades right through the heart of all those somber one-silo towns. Tarpaper shacks on the wrong side of the tracks where moonshiners once brewed sour mash, now labs for their descendants, who cook meth. A black man behind a feed store tossed bales of hay into the bed of a pickup and a few stray Latinos shuffled down the sidewalks, but most of the faces were pasty white. An occasional Stetson. In the window of a thrift store, a tidy row of steel-toed boots.

One day at the commune, his dad returned from a supply run with a film projector and a six-foot screen he had borrowed from an old friend in Baker City. Under a bowl of stars he set up the screen and threaded through the projector a grainy print of *The Bridge on the River Kwai*. Someone filled a hookah with hashish. Someone else balanced foil bags of popcorn on top of one of the campfires. A cooler stocked with cans of cold beer appeared.

Oddly, for one so young, the boy became obsessed with attrition, disintegration, decay. Aiming his Canon at the slow sweep of the Powder River, he noted how the bank kept eroding back into the water one inch at a time. In the community garden, tomato vines hung limp and fruitless, morning frost sparkled in the stubble, the corn stalks died. All of which pointed, in the boy's increasingly cynical imagination, to the planet's inevitable demise. Fallow gardens, abandoned communes, a bridge's shattered timbers splashing into the River Kwai.

In October, chevrons of geese passed over bearing south, a signal for a larger migration the boy would meticulously record: the dissolution of the commune, the attrition of time. Day after day he aimed his lens at the bare clothesline, backpacks stacked next to the fire pit, half a dozen folded teepees lying flat on the ground. Then he moved in for the close-ups: books and posters, Tarot cards and I Ching coins, bundles of sandalwood incense stuffed inside a cardboard box loaded, teetering, into the back of a Volkswagen van.

Quinter. Ellis. Hays. Blue clouds over deep blue hillsides. Crooked tombstones in a pioneer cemetery leaning against the wind.

Once, as he jogged along the river on his usual morning run, the boy heard the members of an apocalyptic splinter group, a clique inside a clique, describe the dark days ahead when the rains would end and the rivers would run dry and the anointed would be lifted into the sky on golden chariots. But even at fourteen he knew that this was nonsense, the bizarre language of peyote buttons choked down with a few ripe slices of locally grown pears.

Although they were both too high to rationally discuss it, the night he watched *Paper Moon* with Dieter they were surprised, and pleased, with Bogdanovich's decision to shoot Kansas in black and white, to let the camera linger on faces as weathered as a prairie barn. The preacher at the funeral, the old lady in the mercantile, the barkers at the carnival where Ryan O'Neal picked up Trixie and sealed, much as Chance had, his tragic romantic fate.

Salina, Junction City, Abilene. Cattle country, pastures shining in the sunbreaks, steady plumes of poison rising from a row of ghostly smokestacks perched on the broken shoulders of a dead-end town.

faye

They ate lunch at the Saratoga, just like they used to when she was a kid. Easing open the front door, Bob Lindstrom nodded at a few of the businessmen at the tables, and the men nodded back, staring curiously at Faye. Some of them, he assumed, had already heard the news—it was impossible, in a town like Terre Haute, to keep something like that secret—and were probably wondering if this was, indeed, the prodigal daughter. Fortunately the men were acquaintances or business associates, not close friends. And even if tonight they would no doubt say to their wives, So guess who I saw at the Saratoga today? and the wives would reply, How did she look? or My God, can you imagine? they were too polite and respectful not to honor the privacy of a family that had already suffered more than its share of grief. And yet despite the patrons' admirable refusal to approach them, Bob couldn't help but notice his daughter's anxiety, the way her eyes darted back and forth across the restaurant before settling, uneasily, on the menu. Abruptly, she slid out of the booth.

Order for us, will ya Dad? I gotta go to the ladies.

But I don't know what you want.

Anything, she said. Whatever you're having's fine.

She wished she didn't have to cross that room—it was like running a gauntlet—but she had no choice; her bladder remained unpredictable these days, another manifestation, she supposed, of her emotional distress. And even though she was clean now, her body was also still rebelling against withdrawal: aching muscles, hypertension, fatigue.

On the other hand, except for a mild case of oral herpes, she had been pleasantly surprised, pleasantly shocked, when the doctor at the clinic, flipping through his chart, informed her that she didn't have any of the dire sexual diseases she had feared the most. Not syphilis, not gonorrhea, not chlamydia. A relatively clean bill of health in the wake of what Mestival had forced her to go through—in the glare of klieg lights, with multiple partners—didn't seem possible, but the doctor was quick to assure her that the test results were accurate. Because of Faye's *special circumstances*, he murmured, averting his eyes, they had run the tests twice. Apparently until something else killed her, she was going to live.

She picked at her pork tenderloin sandwich and too-salty fries, nodding emphatically when her father asked her if she remembered coming here as a child. Of course, she answered, her voice too quick, too bright, too cheerful; ironically, she sounded like her mom. She lowered her eyes, trying to remain calm by concentrating on the sandwich, on the disks of red onion and beefsteak tomato perched, precariously, on that slice of breaded pork. But it was no use, she was fooling herself. The other diners might pretend that she was just another daughter out having lunch with dear old Dad, but she wasn't. She was a circus act, a freak show. Everywhere she went, people gawked.

All she wanted to do today was assure her father that the reason she was leaving Terre Haute again had nothing to do with him and Blanche. That she was fleeing not her parents but her past. To restart their conversation, which had skidded to a stop, she mentioned some of the other restaurants he used to take her to when she was a child. Ambrosini's. The Horseshoe Club. And the A&W on Wabash, she added. You know, the one with the metal bear?

What metal bear?

The one you shot with the plastic rifle. The one Hannah used to get so mad at when it hid behind the bush.

He grinned, remembering. A nickel for three shots, right?

She bit into her sandwich and swirled a french fry in a pool of ketchup, suddenly ravenous. Her appetite had been erratic at best since she came back home but now that she had announced to her startled parents that she would be leaving again in a couple of days, for Florida this time, she was feeling a little less anxious. At least for a few months she wouldn't have to go to places like this, places where, at any minute, an old friend like Cathy Mapes at Baesler's Market the other day might saunter through the door.

Her father looked around the room at the other diners bent like penitents over their plates. Locals. Natives. The same people who had been coming to this restaurant for years. Growing up in Terre Haute he was accustomed to seeing familiar faces in familiar places, but the lack of privacy in a small town, which he once considered a blessing, now seemed like a curse. He tossed his napkin down on the plate. Like Faye, he felt the eyes of the other diners covertly watching him.

I've got an idea, he said.

What's that?

Deming Park. Let's drive out to Deming Park.

When the day was bright and breezy and the joy of spring lingered in the air, when the red-winged blackbird's *deet deedle weet* carried with it the yearly promise of a second chance, when you caught a glimpse of children playing on the swing-sets or a father swatting lazy fly balls to his son, you could hop on one of the miniature train cars and ride the *Spirit of Terre Haute* alongside your father through Deming Park. And afterwards, you could hike up and down the low hills, eventually circling back to the pond where two boys fished for bluegills, their fiberglass poles clinched in the forks of a pair of stubby tree limbs stabbed into the ground, their empty stringers dangling in the muddy shallows. You could walk in the patchy sun through the shadows of beech and maple watching mallards paddle, in no particular hurry, across the windblown waves. And for a while you could pretend that none of it ever happened, that you had never ventured down to Mexico in the first place. But then insistently, inevitably, the ache of melancholy would return, the sadness of spring deep in your bones now, and you would lapse into silence once again.

Fuck it, her father said (and Faye was too startled to respond, too bewildered to reply, because she had never heard him use that word before and never imagined she ever would). The boys lassoed their lines into the waves. Like small green sailboats the mallards turned their backs to the wind and let the momentum of the gusts ruffle their feathers and push them toward the middle of the pond. Daddy?

Fuck it, he repeated. Let's go have a drink.

He chose a dark, cramped lounge on Wabash. A drinker's tavern. An alcoholic's refuge. Blinds closed tight against the daylight. A bartender with a heavy hand. Indicating a booth along the far wall—somewhere they could talk, he said—Bob asked her what she would like.

A beer, she answered. How about a glass of beer.

Apparently it was going to be a day of firsts. She had never heard her father use profane language and she had never seen him touch a drink—he ordered a scotch and soda—before five. But that was okay, because unlike the Saratoga she felt comfortable there. Scanning the sports page, the bartender ignored them while the only other customer, an elderly gentleman sitting alone at the counter gazing down at his glass of whiskey, barely glanced up when they came through the door. Like the bartender, the old man had no idea who Faye was, and she took solace in his vast indifference to anything but his next sip of rye.

Then her father, after a bracing taste of scotch, set his drink down and focused on his troubled daughter, and whatever comfort that dark, anonymous tavern had initially provided was abruptly snatched away.

I want you to tell me about it, he said.

It was as if he had punched her in the gut, blowing the breath out of her lungs. She hung her head in fear, in shame. There was no way she could do this, absolutely no way. If she described the worst of it—the men in masks doing unspeakable things to her—he would likely recoil in horror, blanch with anger, or start to cry. Her voice was tiny, a frightened squeak.

Please, Dad.

About Florida, he said. I want you to tell me about Florida.

Overcome with relief, and deeply grateful to her father for honoring their unspoken agreement not to talk about Mexico—at least not now, maybe later but not now—she described her phone call with Dieter.

He's a writer.

Right. A writer.

And he has a house in Florida.

In the panhandle, she replied. A town called Crooked River. He spends his winters there.

And his summers?

In Bloomington.

Indiana?

Yeah. That's where he's from.

For a split second her father's stern expression, those knitted brows, relaxed.

A Hoosier, huh.

Born and bred, she answered with a touch of pride.

And he's married?

Married, with a boy, a stepson. His first wife—we were good friends in Mexico—his first wife . . . She took a moment to gather herself. Jen's death was still hard to fathom, much less accept. His first wife, she finally admitted, died.

Good lord. Bob shook his head in sorrow, staring at a row of bottles on a shelf behind the bar.

Down there?

No, here. Outside Bloomington. A drunk driver.

Unwilling to dote on the tragedy, Faye took a sip of her beer. Life goes on, she thought. What a silly, hackneyed phrase. And yet technically, of course, it was true.

So this Dieter, you knew him . . . Bob kept his eyes on his drink, trying to figure out how to formulate his next question . . . You knew him from before.

He was in the village, Dad. Those first couple years. We were friends, close friends.

And he wants you to watch his house. To house-sit.

Dog-sit too. They have a Lab, a yellow Lab.

For three months.

Actually, closer to four.

Bob twirled his drink, clinking the cubes against the glass.

It'll be hot you know.

One day, she thought, I'll explain to him how happy I was in that village. How content to work as a waitress in the hotel cantina serving breakfast to the divers who came down for the reef. One day I'll describe the bonfires on the beach, the fishing boats drifting back to the docks, filets of fresh pompano grilled over a bed of native wood. Before Pablo Mestival showed up. Before everything went wrong. She smiled, ruefully.

I guess I've gotten used to that, she said. To the heat.

Well I suppose you can get used to anything. Practically anything.

I suppose you can, she agreed, and when her father nodded, trying without much success to return her smile, she knew in that somber moment that even though he didn't like her leaving, didn't like it one bit, he wouldn't stand in her way.

Okay then, he announced as firmly as he could. That's it then.

But Faye wasn't ready to leave just yet. The glass of beer had emboldened her.

Look, Dad, I know how hard this is for you, and how worried you are. But I'll be all right. I'll be fine.

I know you will.

I really will.

I know it.

The thing is, being back here, back in Terre Haute? It's, it's like . . . She hated her impotence, her helplessness, but how could she possibly make him understand? *Because home is still home*, Parrish muttered, *but you are no longer you.*

As he watched his daughter struggle to find the right words, Bob reached across the table and softly patted her arm, a gesture so tender, so *fatherly* she almost burst into tears. How brave he is, she thought. She had never considered him, this State Farm insurance man, particularly courageous, but all of a sudden she realized how much strength it must have taken for him to cope with a missing daughter, to remain steadfast in the face of such an unthinkable tragedy not for himself but for Blanche, for Hannah, for all of them. She lifted her glass for a toast.

Here's to us, Daddy. Here's to you and me.

Yes, to us, he responded, clicking his glass against hers. To you and me.

blanche

That evening Faye began to pack. Khaki shorts, a bathing suit, her peasant blouses. Sandals and a sun hat. Since Mexico had more or less weaned the idea of vanity out of her system, she was determined to dress for comfort, not style, from now on.

She added a few novels to her suitcase, books she had read back in high school, classics her mother had refused to get rid of when Faye disappeared. *The Catcher in the Rye*, *To Kill a Mockingbird*, *Gatsby*. Perhaps in Florida, unlike in Terre Haute, she would remember how to lose herself in those pages.

On the phone Dieter had described, with a novelist's precision, his home, and now she pictured the details once again. A front sidewalk dividing two squares of lawn. Live oaks, flowering hibiscus, and a pair of century plants—like the ones down in Mexico—on either side of the walk. Old-fashioned white pillars framing the front portico and a solid mahogany door with half a dozen panes of leaded glass opening into the front hallway. A winding staircase to the right.

Her upstairs bedroom was roomy and comfortable, he said, with a twin bed, a walnut armoire, and a window looking down on the pool, the patio, and the truck garden where Maggie grew melons and okra and the strings of chili peppers she used in her homemade salsa.

Either he or Maggie or both of them took Sunny the yellow Lab for walks twice a day. Usually to the town plaza and back but sometimes out to the beach on Christopher Key, where they unhooked the leash and let her run free. If Faye ever wanted to go for a swim in the Gulf, Sunny would be glad to accompany her.

And there was no need to worry, he assured her, if anything unexpected happened at the house, if a faucet started to leak or the air conditioner went on the fritz. He would leave her a list of trusted workmen, a plumber and an electrician and a handyman who occasionally did small repairs. And when she got to town he would introduce her to Lureen, Maggie's younger sister, who lived nearby and would be glad to periodically check up on her to make sure that everything was okay.

It sounded ideal, the perfect place to recover her balance, her equilibrium. Even though she didn't plan to become a recluse, when she wanted to be alone she could be alone, charring a red snapper on Dieter's adobe grill or lounging by the pool on a hot summer day, tropical drink in hand, reading about Atticus Finch.

She closed the suitcase and snapped the locks and set it on the floor. Then she went over to the window to look down on the sycamore, Tanoos's corner market, the modest homes and cracked sidewalks and cars new and old that lined either side of the street. Somehow she had survived Mexico, and now must find a way to survive Terre Haute. A thousand times in Quintana Roo she had given up hope but tonight (and the night after, and the night after that) she would cling to the idea, to the possibility, however faint, that in a small town in Florida she might rediscover the woman she once was.

On her last afternoon in Terre Haute she planted spring peonies with her mother and then, after dinner, sat out on the porch swing with her drinking iced tea.

As usual, Blanche put her brave face on, chatting lightheartedly about Faye's trip to Florida, as if she were a teenager leaving in the morning for summer camp. She was sure, she said, that Crooked River was lovely. And authentic, she'd been told, a genuine fishing town. Just as she was sure that Faye would love it there. The peace and quiet, the boats in the harbor, the smell of the sea.

After Faye went to bed, Blanche lingered for a few more minutes on the porch swing. The streetlamps blinked on over Tenth Street and the air turned pleasantly cool, wafting through the screens. She was sad that her daughter was leaving the next day but happy, too, that she was safe. She had been through hell, and Blanche's heart absolutely ached when she thought about that, but it was time for all of them to move forward, to move on.

A soft breeze purred in the limbs of the sycamore. In a neighbor's backyard a dog began to howl. And down the street a dark blue Monte Carlo eased over to the curb to park in the shadow of a locust's overhanging boughs. If Blanche had been looking in that direction she might have noticed the unfamiliar car pull over to the curb. She might have noticed how, when the engine shut down, the doors remained closed. She might even have noticed the driver, in the temporary glow of an interior light, open up a pocket notebook and thumb through the dog-eared pages, searching for the address of the house he had been sent to by his handlers in Quintana Roo.

chance

He eases the Monte Carlo over to the curb, shuts off the engine, and flips on the overhead light. Thumbs through the pages of his pocket notebook to confirm the address before switching the light back off and rolling down the driver's window so he can read the number on the house directly to his left, 1735. Then checks the addresses on the other side of the street until he finds the one he's looking for.

Like many of the homes on South Tenth Street, 1724 is an older, somewhat dilapidated two-story with green shingle siding and a single dormer window crowning a steeply pitched roof. A towering sycamore dominates the front yard while a row of trimmed boxwood guards the screened-in porch where a middle-aged woman, presumably Faye's mother, rocks back and forth on a porch swing.

Now that he's made it to Terre Haute, now that his target is literally a stone's throw away, his mind drifts back to Valladolid where, a month ago, he received the initial phone call from one of Mestival's subordinates. That handler—Chance didn't recognize his voice—had given him the address of a cantina in Merida. When you get there, he instructed, tell the bartender your name and he'll take care of the rest. Pack for a month of travel, possibly two.

Got it.

Someone will contact you in a few days. Meanwhile, lay low. Eat in the cantina. Drink in the cantina. Sleep there. *Comprende?*

Comprende.

Bored out of his mind, Chance stayed in his uninviting little room above the cantina for the next three days, reading week-old editions of the *USA Today* purchased at a nearby *mercado*. Perched on a threadbare chair next to an open window looking down on a quiet residential street, he scanned stories about the NBA playoffs—the Lakers, led by Magic Johnson, were on a roll—or methodically filled in the daily crossword. Then on the fourth day he answered a knock on the door. Yanking on his boots, he followed the bartender down the dark stairway.

Standing next to one of the rickety tables scattered haphazardly around the room, a middle-aged man wearing horn-rimmed glasses gestured for Chance to sit down. He didn't introduce himself or shake hands, and when Chance offered to buy him a *cerveza*, he refused.

Fine. Have it your way. Chance swung around in his chair to face the bar. *Amigo! Una cerveza por favor.*

After the bartender left the bottle of beer on the table, Señor (not knowing the man's name, Chance would simply call him Señor) leaned forward and spoke in a gravelly voice. His teeth were crooked and his nose, Chance noted, had been broken at least once.

We contacted you because things are, how you say? Unsettled?

Chance nodded, unsurprised. There was always some kind of intrigue. A double cross. A femme fatale. Rumors of betrayal followed, invariably, by rumors of revenge.

Pablo's *puta*, Señor hissed, has disappeared.

Stunned, Chance picked up his bottle then immediately set it back down. He had expected the usual, a stranger's name and the address of his home in Guadalajara. Or the home of his mistress. After he completed the surveillance, developed the photos at the lab in Valladolid, and delivered his report, the blackmail, or in some cases the hit, would be assigned to someone else. It was clean work, sharp and decisive. No guns, no blades, no blood on his hands.

Disappeared?

Escaped.

Good God, Chance thought, how in the world did she do that?

Mr. Mestival, Señor continued, would like to set up a meeting, a one on one. He has a little proposition to make.

Where?

Isla Mujeres.

He had been there once. A white, charmless, boxy safe house with a view across the channel to Cancun.

So when does Mr. Mestival want to meet?

Señor was watching him carefully. Like most of Mestival's thugs, he didn't hide his disdain for gringos. But Chance would not show fear. Even though his nerves were rattled by the news about Angelina, he would not show fear. If they sensed even a trace of weakness, they would eat you alive.

We'll let you know.

Chance nodded; at this stage in the proceedings aggression would be unwise.

Fine. So how long will I be staying here? In Merida?

Señor stood up to leave.

We'll let you know.

When?

For the first time Señor smiled, pleased to ignore the question, to turn on his heel and walk out of the cantina, to show the gringo, in this macho world where a single gesture, misinterpreted, might erupt into sudden violence, his silent contempt.

For years Chance had heard the rumors. Everyone, he supposed, who worked in any capacity for Pablo Mestival—even contractors, independents like himself—had heard the rumors. How after a whirlwind courtship and a year of romantic bliss, something had gone wrong. So wrong that Mestival, in his rage, had chosen not to kill Angelina but to hold her captive. Sometimes the rumors described the drug kingpin catching her in the arms of one of his bodyguards, who was never seen or heard from again. At other times the narrative grew more complex, detailing Angelina's gradual disillusionment with the lover she had not realized, in the throes of her initial obsession, was nothing more than a brutal warlord zealously protecting his kingdom from anyone who might do it harm. At the peak of her disillusionment, it was said, Angelina had lashed out at him, claiming that he was not a real man and that she had been faking her passion all along. In silence, Mestival had seethed, his already unsteady psyche twisted into a knot of rage.

His plan was to exact revenge by making an underground tape that would show Angelina, a woman he once claimed to love, being sexually debased by a group of strangers. But when the film was released on the black market he discovered that dabbling in pornography, at least *this* kind of pornography, was more lucrative than he had imagined. So he decided to produce not just a single tape but a series of them. Prurient viewers—apparently there were legions—were willing to pay a pretty penny for a copy of this type of black-market movie, not so much for the sex, he was told, as for the unwillingness of the woman at the center of all that attention to perform. The more she struggled, the higher the price tag Mestival could demand.

Chance had listened to the rumors with an air of Shaolin detachment. Because none of this would have happened, he reasoned, if Angelina had not rejected him, if she had let him protect her. With his reputation in the surveillance industry firmly established, money would not have been an issue, and they could have lived anywhere they chose. If she wanted to stay in Mexico they could have stayed in Mexico. If she wanted to return to the States they could have returned to the States. Lived in a houseboat on Lake Shasta or a rustic cabin in the mountains of east Tennessee. As long as she was by his side, he would have been willing to go anywhere. But it was too late for that now. Somehow, Angelina had escaped. And in response, Pablo Mestival had a little proposition he would like to make.

He doesn't like the setup. Parking on the street in the dark was standard procedure but tomorrow, in the morning light, the Monte

Carlo would be too conspicuous, too visible to prying eyes. And in a neighborhood like this there were always prying eyes. A busy thoroughfare with a blur of traffic whizzing by wouldn't pose a problem. But tracking the movements of a target from a parked car in a quiet neighborhood was a risky affair.

He twists the key in the ignition and putters down Tenth Street at a snail's pace. And then he sees it, a vacant lot overgrown with weeds directly across the street from Faye's house.

At the end of the block he hooks a left on Hulman then another at the mouth of the alley between Ninth and Tenth. Switching off his headlights, he inches down the bumpy pavement, yanking the steering wheel several times to avoid the deepest potholes, until he arrives at the back of the vacant lot where he stops, shuts off the engine, and climbs out of the car.

It's perfect, a riot of knee-high weeds, a scattering of dandelions, humps of rock and dirt and rubbish. Twin rows of unruly laurel hedges at least eight feet high flank either side of the property, and next to the alley, next to an incinerator for burning trash, someone has abandoned two rusty cars, leaving just enough room between them to squeeze in a third.

Satisfied, he drives back to the Drury Inn. In the shower, he lifts his face to the needles of warm spray and lets his mind leap forward. According to the file, Angelina's father should be a non-factor. An agent for State Farm, he likely spent his weekdays at the office while Faye, still recovering from the trauma of Mexico, no doubt stayed home. Which left only the mother, the wild card. Soaping his chest and arms, he reminds himself not to fret. One way or another it will all work out, because it always does. In the safe house on Isla Mujeres, Pablo Mestival's casual reference to Faye Lindstrom's "elimination" had triggered a wave of self-doubt and nausea. But he's over that now. The assignment is distasteful, even repugnant, but the gods are watching over him, and he's determined not to fail.

Lureen

When the doorbell rang, Dieter scribbled a final note in the margins of the page he was editing and shuffled down the hallway, his flip flops slapping the hardwood floor.

Well hello, handsome, Lureen breathed.

Wearing a tight yellow sundress and wide-brimmed white hat, Maggie's flamboyant evangelical sister leaned in for her usual peck on the cheek while her son Toby burst past the writer, barging through the hallway and out the patio door.

Dieter couldn't help himself, the moment his lips brushed Lureen's cheek his eyes drifted down to the ample cleavage her skimpy dress, the top two buttons wide open, unleashed. Then he abruptly lifted his gaze but not before Lureen registered, with a look of bemusement, his wayward glance.

In the kitchen, Maggie was making a spartan lunch: tomato and feta salad, slices of watermelon, Mason jars of sweet iced tea. Smiling, Lureen bent over for another kiss on the cheek then barked a laugh when her sister, mimicking Dieter, checked out the rosy tops of her breasts.

What? What are you laughing at?

Nothing, Lureen chortled, nothing at all.

Uh huh. Nice dress.

Blissfully unaware of the edge of sarcasm in her sister's voice, Lureen feigned surprise. What, this old thing? Ya really think so?

For a hooker, Maggie mused, holding her tongue. Whenever her sister came over to visit, particularly if she thought Dieter might be home, she always took the opportunity to dress as provocatively as she could. But sometimes, like today, she went too far. That gargantuan garden hat, for instance, looked preposterous. And that cleavage! What in the world must the good ladies of St. Anne's parish think of her?

Ready for lunch?

As long as it's something light, Lureen purred, I'm watching my figure.

In *that* outfit, Maggie drily replied, so is everyone else.

Hunter showed Toby how to toss a quarter into the deep end of the pool then dive down and retrieve it. But Toby was too plump to reach the bottom, so Hunter agreed to switch games.

Cannonball!

Hunter stifled a groan. Cannonball was lame, a game for kids half their age, but he didn't want Toby to brood.

Sometimes Hunter felt sorry for his cousin and the constant battle he fought with his weight. Life was unfair, and Toby's obesity was one more proof of that. Hunter suspected the real culprit was genetics—hefty father hefty son—though God knows Toby's mother didn't have to count the calories *she* consumed. His gaze roved past the pool to the kitchen where Aunt Lureen was leaning over the counter grabbing a slice of watermelon, her *own* melons nearly spilling out of her dress. On the one hand they looked sort of comical, dangling like that. On the other, he wondered why it was so difficult to tear his eyes away.

Cannonball!

Hunter spun around just in time to see his cousin—a white blur, a white blob—smash into the water and spray an alarmed Sunny, who had fallen asleep in the shade of the lemon tree. Whimpering, the yellow Lab skulked away.

Embarrassed by his encounter with Lureen, Dieter returned to his office, softly closing the door. He needed to get back to work, to avoid further distraction, to put his literary house in order before it was too late. For the past few days he had been having a difficult time of it, not writer's block exactly but something just as worrisome, a vague and undefined anxiety when he sat down at his desk to pound out a rough draft of the next chapter. He could blame his lethargy, his lack of a creative spark, on the heat, but it was *always* hot this time of year. He could blame it on Maggie, whose odd behavior the last few weeks had made him increasingly uneasy. Or he could blame it on the new book.

Was it fair for him to write about Faye Lindstrom now that she had miraculously risen, like Lazarus, from the dead? Six months ago the basic premise of a sequel to *Fever Tree* had taken root in his mind. He would follow Angelina as she left the village on the tanned arm of Pablo Mestival. Not knowing what had actually happened to the poor woman, he would then construct a mystery around her disappearance, and by telling her story, her fictional story, illustrate the twin faces of Mexico, the tropical paradise the expats had discovered in Quintana Roo tragically balanced by the dark stain of corruption, exemplified by the flourishing drug cartels, spreading across that proud but unfortunate country.

At first the writing had gone well. Then one morning a few weeks later, thirty pages in, the phone had rung. Dieter gasped, startled to hear Bobby Parrish's voice on the other end. They hadn't spoken in years.

Bobby?

She's still alive, Parrish announced.

Dieter didn't even have to ask who his old friend was referring to. The floor shifted. The walls shook. And in a surge of panic the writer's gaze swept across his desk, freezing on the title page of his newest manuscript, *Flamingo Lane*.

While Toby and Hunter splashed around in the pool, not particularly interested in eating a tomato salad for lunch, Maggie told Lureen that she and Hunter would be flying up to Indiana the following day. Later in the week, Dieter would join them.

Why aren't you all going together?

He wants to make sure the house-sitter gets settled in.

Lureen nodded. Anddddd . . . who is this woman again?

An old friend of his. From Mexico.

An old friend huh.

Maggie didn't bother to reply. In Lureen's world a genuine friendship between a man and a woman was impossible. The sexual component, always present, reigned supreme.

By the way, how come that handsome husband of yours isn't out here eating with us? Did I scare him away?

No, but that dress might have.

Very funny.

Maybe he was worried that he wouldn't be able to stop staring at your tits.

Maggie!

What?

You're always so . . . graphic.

Maggie pondered the word. Graphic? So it was okay for Lureen to casually display her outrageous physical endowments but not for Maggie to use graphic language to describe them?

Am I?

Tits? Lureen whispered.

Sorry, I meant your boobs.

Gee, thanks.

Okay fine. He's working, that's why.

On a book?

Of course on a book. What else?

Lureen hesitated. She didn't want to appear too nosy, or too judgmental (as an evangelical, you had to be particularly cautious about that), but the not-so-subtle clues Maggie had been dropping these last few weeks were too intriguing to ignore.

You know when you say stuff like that—

Stuff like what?

Like what else.

Like what else?

The way you say it, Lureen clarified. It makes you sound a little, I don't know . . .

Defensive?

Yeah, defensive.

Disillusioned?

Yeah, that too. Lureen glanced over at the pool to make sure the boys weren't eavesdropping, then lowered her voice. C'mon, sis, let's have it. What's going on with you two?

In lieu of an answer Maggie considered the lemons drooping from the tree. In a few weeks they would be ripe enough to eat. She saw herself squeezing lemon juice on a grilled flounder while Dieter, sipping a Cabernet, stared off into the distance, no doubt thinking about his book.

Maggie?

What?

Talk to me.

About what?

You know about what. Go ahead. Tell me what's going on.

What she liked most was the lemon's tartness, that little kick at the end. During a silent meal it was something to look forward to. There's nothing to tell, she sighed. There's nothing going on.

Lureen eyed her intently. I see.

No, actually, you don't.

Oh yes I do.

Fine. You see what?

Nothing going on.

Maggie moaned, exasperated.

Is that all you ever think of?

Me!

I didn't say in the bedroom.

You didn't have to!

Maggie stabbed angrily at a wedge of tomato. Like Lureen's sex life was so hot? She visualized good old Charley, Lureen's big oaf of a husband (okay, oaf was a little harsh, Charley was a sweet guy and all, but still) climbing on top of little sister and huffing away. It wasn't a pretty picture.

When he heard a soft tap on the door, Dieter was almost relieved. At this point, anything that might distract him from the roadblocks in the book was welcome. Maggie told him they were taking the boys out for burgers. Then they were all going for a swim.

Where?

Christopher Key. Wanna come?

He did, actually, but he knew he wouldn't allow himself that kind of idle pleasure today.

Sorry, hon, but I gotta work.

Of course you do. What a surprise.

What's that supposed to mean?

It means I want you to tell me—just for fun, okay?—the last time you and I went to the beach.

What is this, Maggie, a pop quiz? He glanced over at the jumble of papers on his desk and wondered why he didn't give in and go with her. Take an afternoon off.

Look, I got work to do, okay?

So in other words *you* can't remember either, she sneered, slamming the door.

As they crossed the causeway to Christopher Key, Maggie gazed out the passenger window at the boats in the harbor chugging south toward Carrabelle. Gathering over the Gulf, a few dark clouds hinted the probability of an afternoon storm. It was early in the season for that kind of activity but she had lived in Crooked River her entire life and she knew the signs. Soon the wind would rise, whipping up the waves. Then the temperature would drop, the clouds break open, the rain hammer down.

Ever since she was a child, this remarkable seascape had surrounded her and she never grew tired of it, the smudges of cloud, the sailboats tacking in the wind, the black shadow of a manatee floating out on the shifting current. The sea, the sky, the causeway connecting the mainland to Christopher Key were in her blood, in her bones. This, she thought, staring out at the harbor, is my DNA. This is who I am.

At the end of the causeway, Lureen turned right, avoiding the overdeveloped southern half of the island for the pristine, protected beaches to the north. On the long straightaway she gunned the engine, cruising past an empty shell of a convenience store with a For Sale sign plastered to its front window, a scattering of summer homes, most of them unoccupied, and the old abandoned saltworks, which lay in ruins now, the crumbling brick walls that once sheltered the evaporation vats tottering in the afternoon sun.

In the north parking lot, the one near the tip of the island, Maggie opened the trunk and retrieved a canvas bag stuffed with towels, sunscreen, and two of Lureen's glamour magazines. Before they sprinted away, she instructed the boys to grab the folding chairs.

They followed the trail into a hushed grove of slash pines, chains of morning glory choking a sandy path framed on either side by prickly pear and saw palmetto, the light broken into mazes by needled boughs. A few hundred yards further on the pines opened up and Maggie saw a brilliant blue canvas strung with ropes of wave. A trio of surfers straddled their boards, facing the open water, waiting for the storm to roll in. A few solitary sunbathers. The usual obnoxious gulls.

Toby and Hunter didn't hesitate. As Maggie and Lureen unfolded their chairs and slathered on the sunscreen, the boys dove headfirst into the waves, gritting their teeth against the initial shock of cold. Hunter caught a rare steep breaker and rode it back to the beach while Toby extended his pudgy arms, content to float on his back and rock in the surf like a buoy.

*

So you agree or not?

Maggie put down the magazine she'd been scanning and looked over at her sister.

Agree about what?

That there's a sex gene.

Watching the boys frolic in the waves, Maggie shook her head in dismay. What in the world are you talking about, Lureen? What sex gene?

The one I heard about on the radio the other day. The one you and I apparently have.

Speak for yourself, please.

Lureen leaned forward, swiping a palm of sunscreen down her calves. I'm just sayin' if there *is* one, then you and I must have it.

Don't be a dimwit, Lureen. Of course there's a sex gene. It's called your libido. And trust me, *everyone* has one.

Well, maybe not everyone.

With her index finger Maggie dragged her sunglasses down the bridge of her nose and stared at the side of her sister's face. And I take it you're referring to . . . ummm, who?

Freshly lathered, Lureen leaned back in her beach chair, basking in the sun. Well for one, she murmured, closing her eyes against the glare, Charley.

Maggie tried not to laugh but lost the battle. Then Lureen started to laugh too.

The clouds were moving in fast now, the wind, the waves. One of the breakers flipped Hunter over and when he came up for air, spitting out a mouthful of saltwater, he saw his mother and Lureen straddling their beach chairs, doubled over with glee. He turned to Toby, who was watching them too.

Whatdya think they're talking about?

Sex, Toby deadpanned. What else?

chance

A few minutes before 8 a.m., Bob Lindstrom left the house on South Tenth Street, unlocked the door of his somber grey Buick, and drove away. Fifteen minutes later, in what Chance assumed must be Faye's second-story bedroom, a light flashed on.

He leaned back in the driver's seat to wait, occasionally activating the windshield wipers to clear the rain that had been falling off and on all morning. At times like this it was important for him to relax, to expand and slow his breathing, but every passing shower that drummed the hood of the car amplified his anxiety. Ever since he woke at the Drury Inn that morning uncharacteristically on edge, he had been battling a case of nerves. Surveillance always included risk—there was no getting around that—but tracking a target from a parked car in a residential neighborhood was particularly tricky. He preferred a room in Puerto Vallarta where he could document, with a telescopic lens, an old-fashioned shakedown or an illicit sexual tryst. But today he doesn't have that luxury. Today he's out in the open. Vulnerable. Exposed.

For the next hour nothing happened, not a single tremor of activity behind the windows of 1724. As the rain slackened, a rusty pickup swished down Tenth Street, a yellow tomcat darted through the wet weeds, a stooped old lady wearing an elaborate head scarf waddled across the road carrying a chafing dish, presumably bound for the corner market at the end of the street. And then, without warning, the front door swung open and Faye appeared, craning her neck to look up at the overcast sky.

Chance thought his heart might stop, his first sight of Angelina since she disappeared from the village four years ago generating a wave of emotions that threatened to drown him. Blind love. The familiar bile of bitterness. Regret. What a beautiful world we could have created. If only she would have accepted me for who I am.

He grabbed the binoculars and focused in on his quarry through the streaked windshield. She was as slender and willowy as ever, but this initial brief glimpse also revealed dark pouches of sleeplessness underneath her eyes as well as strings of uncombed hair spilling down the sides of a face which, in memory, never looked this solemn, never looked this sad.

A few minutes later Faye reappeared in the doorway. With a suitcase in her hand.

Chance flinched. A suitcase? A fucking suitcase? It was the last thing he had expected to see. Why was she leaving? And where would she possibly go?

Holding a folded newspaper over her head for protection from the rain, Faye scurried out to her mother's car, flung open the hatchback, and shoved the suitcase inside. In response, Chance twisted the key in the ignition to activate the manic wipers, which immediately jerked back and forth. Rain pounded the hood again. The wipers cleared the glass. His fingers tapped the dashboard.

He needed to calm down, to reestablish control, to remember the principles of *samadhi*. Concentrate. Disallow distraction. Think it all the way through. She had decided to rent an apartment, a place of her own. Or she was going on vacation. Or she was checking into a detox clinic though surely, since she had been back in Terre Haute for a number of months now that had already been taken care of. Unless, that is, she had suffered a relapse. In the dark weeks following Angelina's abrupt departure from the village, Chance had dabbled in a little heroin himself before enduring a debilitating afternoon of chills and cramps and suicidal fantasies when he quit. So it wasn't hard for him to imagine how excruciating it must have been for her to kick a long-term habit. According to the rumor mill, in order to control his captive, Pablo Mestival had fed Angelina a daily diet of high-grade smack. Until she was all used up. Until she was too listless to perform for a camera or trick out to a friend. Until the drug lord decided that the wisest course of action was to cut his losses by selling her back to her family for what he considered a fair sum.

And then, when the rogue detective the Lindstroms hired to deliver the ransom decided to go cowboy on the deal, the cash exchange had turned into a bloody rescue instead, the man handling the transaction for Mestival, as well as the traitorous bodyguard Sanchez, left dead on the runway of a private airstrip slashed out of a jungle in Quintana Roo.

Not that Mestival, Chance suspected, had actually planned to let Faye go. At the last minute, after the ransom was secured, more than likely an assassin camouflaged by a mesh of trees at the edge of the airstrip had been directed to kill both Faye and her would-be rescuer. But something had gone wrong. And now a traumatized and embittered young woman with far too much knowledge of Mestival's entire operation—the location of his safe houses, the identities of his most vital associates—was out there running loose.

After Faye hurried back inside Chance analyzed, in a lucid state of mind, the situation. Despite the mournful weather and the sudden change of plans, he felt better now that his initial jolt of panic at the sight of Faye's suitcase had subsided. As he shut off the engine to wait for his quarry to reappear, he considered how the gods continued to shine down on him, continued to protect him, like a parent's favorite son. For once again serendipity—one of *their* gifts—had opened a door of opportunity he was more than happy to pass through. If he had arrived in Terre Haute even a single day later, Faye Lindstrom would have already been gone and he would have been left with only one option: to return to Mexico and explain to Pablo Mestival that he had failed. But that hadn't happened, and now he was free to shadow his target no matter where she chose to go.

Filled with newfound confidence he watched Faye, closely followed by her mother, descend the steps, carrying a handbag this time, and when Blanche's Toyota Tercel pulled away from the curb he deftly backed up into the alley and headed north, avoiding the gauntlet of potholes. Pausing at the mouth of the alley, he glanced out the passenger window just in time to see the Tercel swing right onto Hulman, splashing through a puddle of rain.

After tracking them at close range for the first few blocks to gain a sense of Blanche's driving habits, Chance slowed down, staying as far behind the Tercel as he could without losing visual contact. Then, maintaining this safe distance, he followed them up a ramp onto I-70 and settled in for a drive.

Now that the initial burst of adrenaline at the beginning of the chase had begun to wear off, he pressed the fingers of his right hand against his heart again, reassured this time by the slow, steady pulse. At ease, he casually regarded the rural landscape flowing past him, farm country on either side of the highway strangely soothing as it was not unlike the Willamette Valley of his youth. Freshly-plowed fields, old red barns, windbreak poplars. The pewter sky of his childhood. Horses grazing in the rain.

As the latest shower passed over the highway he claimed the center lane, letting his quarry drift out ahead until she almost disappeared. Because a man of his particular talents could tail a target on an interstate, especially an interstate like this one—sparse traffic, ample sight lines—in his sleep.

Corn silos, the flashing lights of an adult bookstore, a drive-in theater like the one in the first shot of *Midnight Cowboy* . . . Finally, on the outskirts of Indianapolis, thicker traffic clotting the road forced him to apply his skills, to smoothly maneuver from one lane to another to match the movements of his quarry. Flipping on his turn signal, he watched a 747 power through the clouds, steadily descending, and it occurred to him that Faye and her mother must be going to the airport. So he pressed down on the accelerator, swinging into the far right lane to close the distance between the two cars. Whatever else happened, he couldn't afford to lose them now.

melissa

At a bakery across the concourse from gate C12, Chance watched Faye hand the gate agent her boarding pass and disappear into the gloom of the tunnel. A few minutes later her plane taxied away, assuming its position at the head of one of the runways. Sipping a cup of lukewarm coffee and tearing off pieces of a stale bagel, he waited a while longer until he was certain that Faye's plane had taken off.

In the parking lot he unlocked the passenger door of the Monte Carlo, flipped open the glove box, and grabbed the prescription vial of Xanax he always carried with him to combat his not infrequent episodes of melancholia.

When the middle-aged woman behind the ticket counter looked up from the update she had just been handed announcing the cancellation of a flight to Minneapolis, she saw a handsome young man with long blond hair ambling across the terminal, headed in her direction.

May I help you?

Good morn . . . I mean good afternoon.

Good afternoon. May I help you?

Well I hope so—he glanced down at her nametag—Melissa. I'm looking for flight, uh, 'scuse me a sec. Frowning, he fished in the pocket of his sweatshirt and retrieved a scrap of paper while Melissa gave him the once-over. Like many flyers who came through her line, he was dressed for comfort, just this side of slovenly. Corduroy slacks, a green Oregon University sweatshirt with attached hood, black Nikes. He squinted down at the scrap of paper.

So I'm looking for the gate for Flight 322. Wait a sec. Yeah, that's it, Flight 322, Indianapolis to Atlanta.

Flight 322, Melissa hummed, glancing at her screen. Here we are. Flight 322, Indianapolis to Atlanta, gate C12.

C12? Great. Thank you! Chance spun around to leave but the agent's voice halted him.

Hold on a minute, sir.

Yes?

I'm afraid that flight's already departed.

What's that?

Your flight. It's already taken off.

It has?

At twelve-fifteen. Melissa tapped her screen with a red fingernail. Twenty minutes ago. I'm sorry, but that plane's already in the air.

Chance grimaced. I am *such* a space cadet, he groaned. I must have written down the wrong departure time.

Well I'm sorry you missed your flight. If you'd like I could—

No, no, it wasn't *my* flight, it was my sister's.

Your sister's?

Yeah, my sister's. She stayed at my place last night—she always does when she flies out of Indy, she's corporate you know—and the thing is . . . well the thing is she left her pills, her blood pressure pills. He fished through his sweatshirt again, this time retrieving the prescription vial of Xanax, which he rattled at Melissa then quickly pocketed.

Oh my.

Listen, I'm sorry to bother you like this, but could you check for me, make sure she got on the plane?

No bother at all. Melissa leaned over her keyboard, rapidly clicking keys. Your sister's name?

Lindstrom, Faye Lindstrom, he replied, spelling the last name.

Oh yes, here she is. Faye Lindstrom, seat 16B. Indianapolis to Atlanta with a connection to Tallahassee. That the one?

When he heard the ticket agent say Tallahassee, a little light in his brain blinked on. Went dark. Then blinked on again.

Did you say Tallahassee?

Yep.

Well that's the one alright. My sister's company, they have an office there. He rapped the counter with his knuckles and flashed the ticket agent the inauthentic smile he saved for such occasions. Thanks, Melissa, you've been a big help.

Is there anything else I can do? We could call ahead and notify her if you'd like.

No, no, that's all right, you've been very helpful. I'll overnight the pills to Tallahassee. Or maybe she can pick up a refill down there. Anyway, I'm sure it'll be fine. *Gracias*.

Tallahassee? The Florida panhandle? Driving back to Terre Haute, he considers the situation from every angle he can think of, convinced that he's right. Who better for Faye to turn to at a time like this than a trusted old friend?

The next day, finished packing, he lingers for a few minutes at the window of his room at the Drury Inn. For the second straight morning the rain that streaks the glass pummels the cars in the parking lot. Yet in two or three days he'll arrive in the sunshine state where, instead of slashing rain, he'll be greeted by a horseshoe harbor shining in the sun, the open arms of a shrimp trawler draped with glistening nets, the antebellum neighborhoods he read about in Dieter's book.

In the breakfast room, idly munching on a slice of whole wheat toast, he flips open a road atlas and traces his route. Kentucky. Tennessee. Georgia. The dreaded Deep South. The great confederacy. Dolly Parton, Lynyrd Skynyrd, pecan fucking pie. And finally Florida, the end of the proverbial line. Or if all goes well, he muses—and why would it not?—the beginning.

dieter

On the drive from the airport in Tallahassee to Crooked River, Faye asked Dieter if he would mind going by the harbor when they pulled into town so she could compare it to the one she had read about in *Fever Tree*.

Only, he responded, if you listen to my standard disclaimer first.

Your standard what?

Disclaimer. You know, this is a work of fiction? Any resemblance to actual people or places is purely coincidental?

The writer's mock-playful tone reminded her how much he used to enjoy this kind of banter; at one time so did she. That's a good idea, she countered. I mean you wouldn't want a reader to think that a novel about *a guy named Dieter* might be true.

Okay then! He licked the tip of his index finger and pretended to draw the number one in the air. Faye one, he announced, Dieter zero.

She appreciated the repartee. After a clumsy embrace at the airport they had strolled out of the terminal talking about what flyers and the people who picked them up at airports always talk about. How was the flight? Did you have anything to eat on the plane? Are you hungry? By acting carefree they had hoped to establish a pattern that would carry them through the day. Now was not the time to talk about Mexico. Now was not the time to talk about Jen.

She looked out the passenger window at a row of bee boxes in a dark patch of woods. Live oaks strung with garlands of Spanish moss, a murky stream wending through densely-timbered bottomland a few miles north of what the tourist brochures referred to as The Forgotten Coast.

So I'm guessing, she said, that you hear stuff like that all the time.

Stuff like what?

You know, people assuming that everything you write is autobiographical?

Even though it's fiction?

Right, even though it's fiction.

She watched him bite his lower lip, shaping a response. He seemed more introspective than he used to be, less spontaneous, more guarded. She wondered if this, at least in part, was the price of fame.

I suppose, he eventually answered, that it comes with the territory.

And you're comfortable with that? With people like me asking these kinds of questions?

People like you, sure. We're old friends. But others?

Not so much?

Not so much, he admitted.

She had read somewhere that the press considered him a recluse. He rarely granted interviews, and when he did, his answers were determinedly concise. He wanted the books to stand or fall, he claimed, on their own.

The trouble is that some of my readers have the strangest connection with my characters, he resumed. They write these elaborate letters.

Connection?

Investment. They have this emotional investment in my characters even though they know I make them up. And then I fiddle with their presumptions.

By using real names.

By using *some* real names, he clarified. And some false ones. Some real places, some fictional ones.

And they resent that.

Dieter shrugged, genuinely befuddled.

And yet they still read your books!

I know! Go figure, right?

Faye's sudden laugh startled her. When was the last time she laughed?

So why not make it easy on yourself, she suggested rationally, and use all fictional names, all fictional places.

Why not make it all up?

Exactly.

Because fiction, he explained, growing more expansive, is based on experience. On real life. And sometimes the line that separates the two gets a little blurred. Besides, he added with a boyish grin, I like puzzles, I like games.

Puzzles, games . . . There were times when she felt almost whole again. And other times when all it took was a word or two to plunge her back into despair. Mexico, she thought darkly, was the ultimate puzzle, the ultimate game, the ultimate mind fuck. You turned over a rock to plant an ocotillo bush and discovered a tangle of snakes underneath it poised to strike. And yet somehow you survived. In the distance she saw a bridge spanning the harbor and then, as they began to cross it, the spire of a church. And as the bridge lifted them up over the water a swell of energy forced her to grip the armrest to control her sudden fright.

The house was a two-story redbrick colonial located in one of the town's most appealing antebellum neighborhoods, a row of classic southern homes Faye recognized, like the harbor, from Dieter's book. Climbing out of the car, she was struck by a kind of literary déjà vu.

As he led her up the walk toward the four white columns that framed the front portico, he provided a brief history of the home. The original owner, he said, was a wealthy cotton merchant during the boom years before the Civil War. Which means, I suppose, that it was built with blood money. But hey, what are you gonna do? Maggie always loved this place—she grew up a block from here—and when she heard it was for sale, we immediately put in an offer.

He eased open the door to one of the upstairs bedrooms and set her suitcase down next to the bed. Out the window she saw a corner of the swimming pool, a slash of blue.

After Dieter excused himself and went downstairs, she put her clothes in drawers, on hangers, on shelves. Books on top of a roll-top desk. Then, in the adjoining bathroom, she splashed water on her face and brushed her hair and applied a faint streak of lipstick. Since she must look to Dieter like she's aged ten years, the least she could do was make herself presentable.

A little weary from jet lag, she stood at the window looking down at the backyard where Sunny, the yellow Lab, slept in the sun while Dieter cleaned the grill of an adobe oven with a wire brush. Above the rooftops, a small plane floated by.

When she came out to the patio, Dieter asked her if she'd like to take Sunny for a walk. They could go down to the harbor. Or maybe she'd like to rest first? Take a nap?

I'm fine. I'd like to see the boats. And Sunny needs to get used to me, right?

At the end of the block, catching sight of the town plaza, she was struck once again by déjà vu. The long X of sidewalks crisscrossing the center of the square. The furniture store owned, in *Fever Tree*, by Maggie's father. It all seemed so familiar, just as she had imagined it would be. The Gibson Hotel, Blue Moon Tavern, Delta Café: here they all were, straight out of the pages of a book. The only thing that seemed to be missing was Uncle Billy, the old black gardener. And the statue of General Lee.

As they approached the harbor, the sun hovering over the palm trees out on Christopher Key bathed the ships in the marina in buttery light. Dieter suggested a drink. Or coffee, he quickly added. Anything you want.

He's trying to please me, Faye thought, but he isn't sure how to do that, isn't sure how much I've changed. He's wondering if I still drink, still listen to Dylan, still on occasion flash that quicksilver wit, even drier than his, that forged our friendship in Quintana Roo. Smiling to reassure him that she wasn't as fragile as he might assume, she switched the leash to her right hand and looped her left arm through his. She was so glad to see him. In the village, even in those halcyon days when there wasn't much, really, to worry about, he had been her anchor. A drink, she said, sounds wonderful. A drink sounds great.

They sat outside on the deck of The Tides watching the oyster boats and shrimp trawlers return to their berths. Loose clouds drifted seaward. A chevron of pelicans floated, in military formation, over Christopher Key. And in Faye's enchanted eyes the entire scene—the dusky light, the ships in the harbor, the stained clouds—took on the aspect of an old painting. If you lived here, she thought, why would you ever want to leave? I can't believe how beautiful it is, she said. She tasted her chardonnay's slight hint of apple, slight hint of pear. And I can't believe, she added, that I'm here.

Instinctively Dieter reached across the table to squeeze her hand but then, embarrassed by such a blatant gesture of affection, quickly withdrew it. There was so much he wanted to tell her. That he missed her infectious laugh. That he sometimes dreamed about the day she fled the village with Pablo Mestival. That losing her (like everyone else, when she was officially declared missing he had presumed that she was dead) was almost as hard as losing Jen. But he doesn't know how to say things like that anymore. When Jen died, something inside of him died too.

To camouflage his embarrassment he indicated, through the tavern's plate glass windows, a row of drinkers perched like the statues on Easter Island along the perimeter of the bar. See those guys in there? The ones pretending not to look at us? They can't believe you're here either.

Faye stifled a laugh, which woke up Sunny, who had fallen asleep on the deck's warm planks. She leaned down to pet her.

So they figure I'm . . . what? Your mistress? Your sister? A friend?

Those guys are mostly deckhands, okay? Good people. Good solid people. But they're a little jaded too. I'll go with mistress.

Do they know Maggie?

If they grew up around here they do. But the others, no. 'Cause I usually come here alone.

Something about this revelation troubled her. She hid it by playing coy. Your secret hideaway, huh?

Let me tell you somethin', sister, there's nothin' secret about *this* place.

At the mouth of the harbor an oyster boat chugging back to the marina plowed through the pass. So you hang out here, she said.

Sometimes when I'm done writing I go over my notes here, here on the deck. Then I go inside and drink with the boys.

You and the boys.

Me and the boys.

Talkin' baseball.

Talkin' baseball. Fishin'. You know, guy stuff.

The famous reclusive writer, she said with a gleam, hanging out with the great unwashed.

She may have lost her innocence, he thought, but clearly she hasn't lost her wit. The famous reclusive kook, he corrected her. Not writer, kook. They think I'm eccentric.

Who, you? Eccentric? Where in the world would they get *that* idea?

They ordered a platter of oysters, another pint for Dieter, and another glass of chardonnay. Dieter sprinkled a few drops of hot sauce on one of the oysters then forked it out of the shell. From right out there, he said proudly, pointing the tines at the harbor. Probably caught today.

When she asked about the old crowd, Dieter shrugged. Then he mentioned a few names, a fan letter, a recent phone call. From Parrish, he said. Of all people! Oh, and Chance called too. Remember

Chance? Not sure how he tracked me down, but six or seven months ago the phone rang and it was him.

Good God, she thought, Chance? Fucking Chance? It was the last name she had expected, or wanted, to hear. She reached out for a sip of wine but her hand was shaking so badly she was afraid she might topple the glass. The deck seemed to buckle, to sway out over the water. If I stand up now, she thought, I'll fall. Or faint. She gripped the edge of the table, waiting for the dizzy spell that always accompanied her anxiety attacks to pass.

Faye?

In reply, she offered him a sickly smile, which only exacerbated his concern.

Are you okay?

I'm fine, she murmured, fine. Gritting her teeth, she asked him where the ladies' room was, then felt the weight of his worried regard as she stumbled away.

In the restroom she washed her hands, staring at her face in the mirror. Sometimes the voices she used to hear in the courtyard outside her room in the hacienda where they shot the movies abruptly returned. A cameraman discussing close-ups. The guy in charge of the lighting complaining that the new bulbs weren't up to par. One evening she heard two of the maids talking about Chance. They were speaking in Spanish but she was still able to decipher the gist of what they said. In some capacity, she wasn't sure exactly what, it seemed that Chance was working for Pablo Mestival. The two women referred to him as *a contractor*. But how could that be, she had wondered, how could that possibly be? How could someone like Chance work for such a monster?

She snapped a paper towel out of the dispenser and dried her face. Her heart was still pounding but after a few minutes she began to calm down. Ever since she fled—escaped—Mexico she had become accustomed to these occasional bouts of panic. The only option, she had discovered, was to let them run their course, which usually didn't take long. The episodes were frightening, even debilitating, but thankfully brief.

Sorry, she mumbled.

Dieter looked up at her with such concern and affection she thought she might cry. She thought they both might.

I have these spells.

No worries, he said.

This time, when he squeezed her hand he didn't let go.

chance

Heading south out of Terre Haute, he cruises past cornfields, chicken coops, Shakamak State Park. Past a rifle range, stone quarry, battered blue pickup straight out of a demolition derby riding the smooth wake of an unblemished Cadillac Seville.

Hoosiers on the loose on a damp Sunday morning. Bound for church. Or a tractor pull.

Ground zero. The fabled heartland's straight-as-a-staff backbone on full display. Bible thumpers, feed stores, flags at half-mast. Nixon's silent majority? Apparently this is where they live, and Chance the contrarian figures that maybe he should too. Get back to the land. Wake up in the morning and milk a cow. Catch a catfish. Shuck an ear of corn.

Is it too late for him to change the outcome that now seems inevitable? Is there still time for his karma to kick in? An upbeat conclusion seems highly unlikely, requiring the kind of improbable fictional twist even a writer as imaginative as Dieter would surely shy away from. Yet it's not that difficult for Chance to imagine Faye in a farmhouse here in the heartland after all of this is over doing . . . what? Churning butter? Baking a rhubarb pie? Glancing out the window as her beloved stacks a cord of wood or fine-tunes the carburetor of what their jovial Swedish neighbors affectionately refer to as his Yon Deere?

A young man with a perplexed expression is standing next to a pickup parked on the shoulder of the road. One of the truck's back wheels is jacked up a foot off the ground but the guy's just standing there with a tire iron in his hand. Did he forget his spare? Chug one too many Bloody Marys for breakfast today? Chance slows, frowning: c'mon, dude, you're a Hoosier, you're supposed to carry a spare. He considers stopping but what would be the point? Visualizing the hayseed's aw shucks gratitude, he stomps down on the accelerator, whipping by.

His own spare is fully pressurized and locked in place. He knows this because he double checked at the Drury Inn this morning when he secured his cleaned and oiled handgun, a Walther .380, behind a false panel in the Monte Carlo's roomy trunk. You're only as good as your tools, his father used to say. But he doesn't want to think about that now. He'd rather shift his Shaolin focus into idle, rather concentrate not on the daunting task ahead but on the image that keeps streaming through his mind: Faye, like his mother, pinning his shirts to a clothesline on the edge of a cornfield just south of the town she once again calls home.

Pulling into the parking lot of a roadside emporium featuring, among other questionable items, log rolls (whatever those are), he flips open the road atlas, props it on the dash, and traces his current route south to I-64 then due east to Louisville. Then south again. Or he could cut over sooner than that on state road 150, which would take him through Loogootee (Christ, what kind of cornpone name is that?), French Lick (hey, isn't that where Larry Bird's from?), and Paoli. He opts for the interstate. The back roads through the heartland have been a pleasant diversion but it's time to move on.

As he follows the circular ramp onto I-64, the rain blows over, the clouds disappear, and wet fields on either side of the highway shine like diamonds in the sudden morning sun. Shifting into cruise control, he slips on his sunglasses, recalling the day he boarded the ferry to Isla Mujeres to meet with Pablo Mestival. Fittingly, the weather on *that* particular morning could not have been less inviting. A steady downpour, ominous thunder, not a sunbreak in sight.

Standing next to a black Lincoln at the landing, Señor squinted through his horned-rims, waiting for the ferry to shudder to a stop. Then he signaled Chance, who hurried across the parking lot, splashing through puddles of rain.

Before he flung open the Lincoln's shiny back door, Señor stared down in disdain at the gringo's muddy boots. In response, Chance smiled sarcastically and said *buenos días,* it's a pleasure to see you again too. Then he slid into the Lincoln and waited, like an honored guest, for his handler to shut the door. *Mano a mano*, he thought. Let the macho dance begin.

The windshield wipers flailed back and forth and the tires sang on the wet pavement as they sped down the coastal road past stretches of rainy beach, the local *aeropuerto*, a pair of tin shacks painted swimming-pool blue. No one was out. No bicyclists on the road. No divers clinging to the ladder of a dive boat. No dive boats.

The safe house on Isla Mujeres was pale, boxy, and charmless. Off-white walls. Open ceilings soaring to nowhere. Narrow windows allowing in too little light.

A woman in her thirties, a no-nonsense business type—readers on the bridge of her nose, a strict blouse and skirt ensemble, sensible shoes—ushered him out to a back deck facing a sandy yard, a sweep of flooded beach, and the turbulent channel he had just crossed on the ferry. The woman indicated one of two patio chairs separated by a small wooden table underneath an eave of plexiglass panels that kept that section of the deck dry. She asked him if he would care for a refreshment and he responded *cerveza, por favor*. Brisk and efficient, she returned in less than a minute carrying a pint glass topped with a finger of foam.

*

An hour south of Louisville, he glances idly out the window and sees a chestnut mare trot across a dusty paddock, a young boy in the shadow of a sturdy Dutch barn twirl a lasso, the delicate whips of a willow sweep the surface of a shallow pond. Horse country. Low rolling hills and lush bluegrass pastures. Elegant ranch houses set back off the highway in the cool shade of maples and elms.

There's something intriguing, and slightly unreal, about such an orderly landscape. Symmetrical hedges, half-moon gravel driveways, freshly painted homes. He pictures Burl Ives sipping a mint julep out on his verandah while the horse trainer and a housemaid scurry out to the stable to get down to business in one of the stalls.

With an ingratiating smile Pablo Mestival waltzed out to the back deck and offered his guest his hand. Chance, my old friend, welcome.

A strong, confident grip, fearless gaze, Zen-like bearing. Fit, fifty, with a military buzz haircut and a black polo shirt open at the collar, the drug kingpin projected casual authority and an aura of myth. Before sitting down, he asked Chance if he would like another *cerveza*, and when Chance said why not, he surprised his guest by going back inside and pouring it himself.

Chance reminded himself to drink moderately. He needed to keep a clear head and should have probably stopped at one, but the beer helped steady his nerves. He took a modest sip and set the glass down. Then he leaned forward and lowered his voice respectfully.

I am sorry, he said, to hear about your troubles. With the girl.

Mestival shrugged, wearily. A sad business, my friend. A sad affair.

Naturally his first glimpse of Nashville's skyline reminds him of Dylan. And naturally this makes him blue. *Nashville Skyline* was one of the handful of albums Angelina brought with her to Mexico, and on those rare occasions when Chance was invited to her and Jen's house at the edge of the village it wasn't unusual to hear *Lay Lady Lay* playing in the background. He recalls the photo on the back cover, the same grey buildings he's looking at now.

Irritated, he punches buttons on the radio, one country crooner after another, until he fastens onto Tom T. Hall. That's what *I'm* talkin' about, he mumbles: old dogs and children and watermelon wine. Roots music. Americana. Songs that passed the test of time. Even the hippies on the Powder River, whose musical tastes ran toward psychedelia, raved about this stuff. Cash and Haggard, Chet Atkins, Doc Watson, Patsy Cline.

When Mestival announced his proposal, Chance the samurai refused to buckle. No worries, his inner voice cautioned. No sweat.

Relaxed now that his cards were on the table, the kingpin gazed across the rainy channel at the lavish hotels of Cancun rising, like pale monsters, out of the gouged land. Of course this little problem of yours, he announced breezily. . . Well, let's just say when you come back from your visit up north that little problem will no longer exist.

Gracias, Señor.

De nada, Mestival replied. One hand, how does it go, washes the other?

Chance smiled, weakly, his *little problem* weighing on his mind. How, he wondered not for the first time, had his initial, seemingly harmless flirtation with gambling spun so quickly out of control? It had started out as nothing more than a diversion, a Saturday night lark. Casual bets on a jai alai match in Tijuana. A small wager on the Super Bowl. Occasional cock fights. Yet only a blind man would fail to see how those innocuous early forays led to his eventual downfall at a poker table in the back room of a cantina in Oaxaca. Blackjack. Texas Hold'em. Five-card stud. How many times could you double down in a single fucking night? Eventually, on a busted flush, he lost it all. And more.

Bewildered by the enormity of what he had just done (or more precisely, undone) he had stumbled back to his hotel and drifted into fitful sleep, only to wake a few hours later with an overwhelming sense of dread. He was deep in Mestival's pocket now, the last person on the planet you wanted to owe.

On the back deck the kingpin turned the full glare of his smile on his guest. But Chance wasn't fooled by that glitter of fangs.

Elimination, sí?

Sick at heart, Chance replied, *sí*.

After wolfing down a mediocre plate of sweet and sour chicken at an Asian restaurant just off the highway, he follows the ramp back onto I-75. But the food does not sit well. He feels weak and nauseated and a little afraid. What if the chicken he just ate was undercooked and he has food poisoning? Or worse, salmonella. He winces, his stomach muscles a tangle of cramps, wondering why in the world he had thought a Chinese restaurant in Cordele, Georgia was a good idea.

Up ahead he spots a sign for a cluster of motels and flips on his blinker. Salmonella? Really? More likely the root of his indigestion is the interminable drive and the stress of the assignment. Or maybe in the back of his mind he's more worried about Faye Lindstrom than he cares to admit. What if she didn't go to Crooked River after all? What if she has a friend in Tallahassee she plans to visit instead?

There were too many unknowns, too many variables. What if Dieter isn't even in Florida? Didn't the writer tell him on the phone a few months ago that he spent part of the year up north? He snaps a right at the bottom of the off ramp and gasps. Cold chills. More cramps. A jolt of fear. If he loses her, he's not sure he can face Pablo Mestival again. Because the Capo would never forgive him, he's certain of that. He would give him an ultimatum, a matter of weeks to pay off his debt or face the dire consequences. As he clings to the steering wheel with sweaty hands, another wave of cramps doubles him over. No, if he fails, he won't be able to go back to the Yucatan. But how could he make a living anywhere else? If he puts out feelers, Mestival will likely hear about them and send one of his flunkies to finish him off. He jerks the wheel hard to the left and swerves into the parking lot of the first motel he comes to. The bottom line is simple: he has to quit wasting his time on idle fantasies and face the brutal truth. His fate is sealed. If Faye Lindstrom isn't in Crooked River, he's fucked. And if she is, he'll have no choice but to complete his stomach-churning task.

Elimination, sí?

Sick at heart, Chance replied, *sí*.

faye

The morning after Dieter left to drive up to Indiana, Faye woke refreshed and reinvigorated and ready for the first time since her escape from Mexico for whatever the world decided to throw her way. She had slept surprisingly well for a change, and she couldn't help but consider this a good omen. Sitting up in bed with her back against the headboard, she looked out the window at the curved canopy of Dieter's lemon tree and the gabled roof of the house next door.

Except for the faint tick of a grandfather clock down the hallway, the house was pleasingly silent, and she felt safe and comfortable there. In Terre Haute she always woke too early, listening to her father downstairs getting ready for work or her mother in the kitchen making breakfast. Sometimes she tried to drift back to sleep but almost always in vain. Ever since she kicked her habit, her mind tended to race in the morning, just as it did when she woke up—and she woke up often—in the middle of the night. Crippled by insomnia, and haunted by yet another frightening dream, she would drag her body out of bed, already exhausted.

But this morning, after ample rest, her resolve to stop obsessing about the past and get on with her life after Mexico has returned. She's alone here, truly alone for the first time in years, and she suspects that this is exactly what she needs for the healing process to begin. She hears a series of thumps and looks over at Sunny furiously bumping her tail against the door frame, waiting for her new master to get out of bed.

*

Downstairs she fills Sunny's bowl with dry chow and sets it out on the flagstone patio. Then she conducts a quick inventory of the pantry and fridge. The pantry is well stocked but the refrigerator mostly empty. Rifling through a junk drawer next to the stove, she finds a pad and pencil and starts to jot down a grocery list. Then she sees the note Dieter left for her on the counter. The name and phone number of his handyman, in case anything goes wrong. Directions to Winn-Dixie, the post office, the library, and a nearby video store. And of course the writer's phone number up north. *Call me anytime*, the note concluded, *even if you just want to chat. And have fun! Love, Dieter.*

As she finishes the grocery list she recalls how in Mexico, during the good weeks when Mestival was away, she had often thought about Dieter and sometimes wondered if she would ever see him again. After the rescue, when Hannah described his success as a writer, Faye had been delighted if not particularly surprised. Back in the village there had been no doubt in her mind, or anyone else's for that matter, that one day he would publish his work to acclaim. He was too talented, and too dedicated to his craft, to fail. I'm so happy for him, she cried. Then she saw a shadow cross her sister's face and instinctively recoiled. Softening her voice, Hannah told her about Jennifer, and Faye's delight immediately vanished. How could such a thing happen? A head-on collision? Instant death? Poor Dieter. Poor Jen.

Drying her eyes, she claps her hands twice and waits for Sunny to trot into the kitchen. Shopping can wait. It's time for their morning walk.

As she crosses the central plaza she notices three or four tables set out on the sidewalk in front of a bakery called BJ's, so she heads in that direction. Clipping Sunny's leash to a chair leg, she slips inside and orders a cup of coffee and a blueberry muffin from a young woman wearing a tie dyed T-shirt and a paisley headband. Faye didn't know young women still dressed that way. I like your shirt, she says.

The girl's smile is radiant, revealing two rows of pearly teeth. Her name, according to a tag pinned to her shirt, is Sarah.

Thank you. I like your dog!

Faye glances out the window at Sunny waiting obediently next to the table. Actually, she confesses, she's not mine.

Sarah's eyes widen. She looks confused.

It's a friend's, Faye quickly adds. I'm housesitting for him. And taking care of his dog.

Visibly relieved, Sarah hands Faye her mug of coffee and blueberry muffin. Sweet! It's a Lab, right?

Yep.

I used to have one, a chocolate. She nods out the window at Sunny. He was just like yours, she says, mellow.

Smiling, Faye turns to leave—she wants to drink her coffee in the morning sun—but Sarah's voice stops her.

That house you're watching, it's around here?

Yep. Faye points, vaguely, to the north. Just a couple blocks away.

Nice. So what's your name anyway?

Faye. My name's Faye.

Once again the dazzling smile, the shiny teeth. Well I'm Sarah. See ya next time, Faye.

Outside she sits down at one of the tables, feeling a little shaky. Sarah's simple gesture of kindness has unnerved her, and she looks at Sunny for the second time that morning through a sudden blur of tears.

The sky is clear and the sun, peeking over the roof of the Gibson Hotel, pours light down on the plaza and its handful of pedestrians, on this quiet Sunday morning, out for their morning stroll. Faye takes a sip of the rich black coffee and sighs, contented. At peace. Dare she even think it? Happy?

Striding past her table, an elderly gentleman wearing an old-fashioned seersucker suit and a sky-blue bow tie bows his head and wishes her a formal good morning, and as she watches him cross the street and disappear inside the Gibson it occurs to her that this elegantly dressed southern dandy might be Mr. Gold, the genteel hotel manager in *Fever Tree*. She takes a bite of her blueberry muffin. Mr. Gold! She isn't sure if the eccentric old manager has just stepped out of the pages of a book, but how pleasant it is to consider that possibility. After all, she muses, isn't that what each of us, deep down, desires? To live in a storybook? Even if, according to Dieter, the story isn't true?

As Faye pushes her cart down the brightly-lit aisles of Winn-Dixie, she considers how much more relaxed she feels today than she did when she went grocery shopping with her mother at Baesler's Market. In memory, that afternoon has taken on the aspect of an unsettling dream, her mother scurrying down the aisles in a manic rush, the garish lights and colors assaulting Faye's senses, and finally the bizarre encounter with her former schoolmate next to the kosher pickle display. In contrast, Winn-Dixie seems like an island of calm.

She glances down at the list in her hand and begins to pile items into her cart. A box of spaghetti, a few links of Italian sausage, a bottle of chardonnay. On a whim, she adds a small package of Belgian chocolates and a pint of cherry ice cream. A loaf of bread, container of yogurt, quart of low-fat milk.

At the checkout counter a matronly cashier with curly white hair pauses for a moment as she rings up the chocolates. She glances covertly at Faye and lowers her voice, like an old friend sharing a delicious secret. I love these things, don't you? Trouble is, they're addictive. The cashier swivels her gaze around the store, as if to make sure that no one's listening. I buy a package like that? Wouldn't last a day!

While the marinara sauce gently bubbles in a saucepan on the stove, Faye decants the bottle of chardonnay, goes out to the patio, and flips open her paperback copy of *To Kill a Mockingbird*. Her gaze descends the first page, that famous opening sentence—*When he was nearly thirteen, my brother Jem got his arm badly broken at the elbow*—triggering a memory of reading these same passages out on the porch swing on South Tenth Street on a summer afternoon when she was what, sixteen, seventeen? It seems like a lifetime ago, and in a way, she supposes, it is.

After finishing the first chapter she lights the tiki torches on the corners of the patio then stirs the hot coals beneath the grill of the adobe oven and carefully lays an Italian sausage on top. In the kitchen, she whisks the marinara sauce before returning to Atticus Finch.

One day in the hacienda west of Tulum she told Sanchez, the only one of Mestival's bodyguards who appeared sympathetic to her plight that she liked to read. Mestival was in Oaxaca on business that month, which meant that there would be no more filming until he returned. And while it was a blessing not to have to face the camera for a while, there was little for her to do. She walked with Sanchez in the morning, shot up in the afternoons, slept through the heat of the day. Sometimes she helped the cook make dinner or the gardener prune his orchard of avocado trees or the maid cull the strings of chili peppers hanging from the eaves of the veranda. Sometimes she sat in the shade of the jicaro tree in the courtyard idly flipping through the pages of one of the cook's glossy magazines. But at night, confined to her room, she was bored stiff.

A few days later Sanchez knocked on her door. He was carrying a stack of paperback books: Carlos Fuentes, Gabriel García Márquez, Octovio Paz. And when she finished those, he brought her a second stack, American mysteries this time: Ross Macdonald, Dashiell Hammett, John Dickson Carr. She thanked him for his kindness and kissed him on the cheek and in response he shyly lowered his eyes, a gesture so tender she wondered if he might be developing a crush. One of the maids at the hacienda had told her that Sanchez recently lost his wife to breast cancer. Grief stricken, he must have ached for female companionship, for someone to fill that romantic void. And there she was, a fellow sufferer.

One morning as he waited to escort her on their daily walk across the savanna, he abruptly turned his back when she lifted off the negligee she had slept in and started to dress. It hadn't crossed her mind that anyone in that awful place might be modest, much less chivalrous, and she was immediately sorry that she had disrobed like that in front of him.

Now she pours a second glass of wine and sits down to eat. The pasta is delicious but her sad recollections have ruined her appetite. Without considering the consequences, Sanchez had offered her protection and lost his life in return. And I'm the one, she tells herself for the hundredth time, who's to blame.

She stabs at a chunk of Italian sausage swimming in the marinara sauce and angrily chews it to a pulp. I'm not going to keep doing this, she vows, not going to keep blaming myself for the bodyguard's death or my own debasement. Like her, Sanchez crossed paths with a monster and paid for that horrible twist of fate with his life. A little calmer now, she refocuses on her meal. No matter how deep her sorrow, this time she's determined to resist the urge to cry.

chance

He sleeps, wakes, broods. Twists the bedsheets into knots remembering last night's lousy sweet and sour chicken which may or may not have poisoned him. Recalls the nausea, the blinding headache, the bone-deep chills. Recalls how, doubled over with cramps, he swerved off the interstate into the parking lot of this two-bit motel and collapsed on the bed, shivering.

Stubbing a toe against a chair leg, he staggers into the bathroom and retches, kneeling on the hard tile floor. Rinses his mouth out with lukewarm water then swallows a sip of cold. Stares in dismay at his haggard face in the mirror before switching off the bathroom light, lurching back to bed, and fumbling for the remote control. Infomercials? Christ-on-a-crutch is this all the network gurus in their infinite wisdom can come up with these days to lull insomniacs back to sleep? How to avoid the IRS, construct the perfect salad, restore your thinning hair? Like a dead man, he gazes at the screen without a flicker of emotion.

Sleeps, wakes, frets. Dreams about salad shooters, an audit by the IRS, and a manic sexual episode with Goldie Hawn. On a trampoline. Overlooking a tropical beach. Stumbles back to the bathroom and pops two more Tylenol and a second Xanax. Whiskey. What he needs now is whiskey. Kentucky bourbon. Georgia moonshine. Triple malt scotch.

Tosses. Turns. Tries to catch Goldie as she bounces off the trampoline and sprints, buck naked, toward the sea. Opens his eyes and sees a blush of light behind the closed curtains. Momentarily his spirits sort of lift, then sort of plummet. He's survived the black night of his illness all right but so what? His head is still pounding. He's thrown up three times in the last two hours. And his fever is off the charts.

In the motel lobby he informs the bitter-looking shrew behind the front counter that he'll be staying another day, maybe two. Considers adding that he's sick as a dog but changes his mind. Like he'll get any sympathy from this old bat? Frowning, she contemplates with obvious disdain his tattered green robe and cherry-red flip flops.

Charge it to the card he snarls as he spins on his heel and marches toward the door. Determined to maintain some semblance of dignity, he gives the door a mighty shove then wheels around in dismay as the hem of his robe catches between the door and the jamb, jerking him backwards. Yanking the robe loose, he shoots the clerk a sickly smile, daring her to laugh.

As he crosses the parking lot, he grabs his aching skull with two shaky hands and squeezes. Already the sun is glaring down, bouncing off the windshields like waves of whatever from outer space. On the interstate the driver of an eighteen-wheeler blasts his air horn, and he nearly sheds his toxic skin, nearly dissolves into a puddle right there in the middle of the parking lot of the motel from hell.

Back in his room he sleeps, dead to the world, for the next three hours. Lost in a fever-dream, he watches the Powder River flow past a teepee where his father and a pair of hippie girls engage in erotic gymnastics in the name of harmony and love. Loose clouds over dry hills. Willows dipping their slender fingers into the stream. Casting his fly line into the eddy where trout drowse, the boy lifts his face to the sky . . . and shudders awake in a searing white sunburst of paranoia when he hears a knock on the door, his sole consolation the knowledge that he's holed up in a motel somewhere in the dark heart of Georgia where no one can possibly know who he is.

He cracks open the door and sees a ridiculously young housekeeper balancing in her childlike hands a swaying tower of fresh towels.

Mutters come back in an hour *por favor* and watches her scurry away, clearly relieved. Get it together, his inner voice cautions. Take a hot shower. Wake the hell up.

He tugs on fresh underwear, soiled jeans, an Oregon Ducks T-shirt. Damn near swoons when he leans over to lace up his sneakers then crashes out the door at the same moment the impossibly young maid emerges from the next room dumping an empty pizza box into a trash bag fastened to the end of her cart.

Any time, he croaks.

She backs up, her eyes darting around the parking lot for an avenue of escape.

Any time what?

Any time you wanna clean the room. I'm going now.

In a grocery store called, to his astonishment, Piggly Wiggly, he buys another vial of Tylenol, a container of dry noodle soup, two quarts of ginger ale, a thermometer, and a box of black hair dye. Sliding the box of dye across the scanner, the cashier looks up at him, like everyone else in town, with alarm. He shrugs, says *what*? Says *Piggly Wiggly? Are you fucking kidding me?*

Instinctively, like the maid that morning, the cashier retreats a step, bumping her hip against the cash drawer.

At the motel he slips a coin into a newspaper box and fishes out a copy of *USA Today*. Waves at the scowling desk clerk tracking him across the parking lot like he's some kind of circus freak, the boy with three hands.

The room is neat and orderly now but cold chills still rack his body and his temperature has climbed to 103. Shivering, he dry swallows two more Tylenol, leaves his clothes in a heap on the floor, crawls under the covers, and loses consciousness in no time at all.

At dusk he heats the noodle soup in the microwave, takes a few sour sips, and trashes it. Uncaps the bottle of Jim Beam he bought that morning at a nearby liquor store and pours two fingers, neat, into a flimsy plastic cup. There, that's better: when in doubt, drink. In underwear and T-shirt he slumps in a ratty armchair nursing his glass of whiskey and scanning the paper for items of maniacal behavior that might provide a little comic relief. Like this one about the Spaniard who attempted to assault Pope John Paul II with a bayonet (try a gun next time, idiot). Or the war, if you want to call it that, in the Falklands. The fabled British Empire battling the combined military forces of . . . Argentina? Really? Another gulp of whiskey and his mood suddenly lightens. Is it possible that the flu or the food poisoning has peaked? Or is that the whiskey talking?

Drifts. Rouses. Twists the bedsheets into knots. Screws Goldie Hawn one more time then wakes in the middle of the night in tears though he isn't sure why. Something about a dream. Something about his mother. Spies the fifth of Beam on top of the dresser, half empty.

Every muscle in his body trembles and aches but at least he's stopped throwing up. Rallies. Fades. Sleeps undisturbed for two more hours then wakes on a cloud of soft morning light feeling terrific. Climbs out of bed stretching his back muscles, his neck muscles, Sufi-whirling his arms. Palms his forehead, which is cool and dry.

In the bathroom he tears open the box of black hair dye and follows the directions and forty-five minutes later emerges from his room into what feels today like gentle sunlight glowing down on the outskirts of a quaint southern town. Whistling, he flings his duffel into the trunk, goes inside to settle the bill, and on his way out gives the scowling clerk a sarcastic thumbs-up just to prove that she's an old bat and he's a man on the go, baby, who doesn't have time for downers like her.

The clerk can't believe her eyes. It's the worst dye job she's ever seen. And she's seen some real doozies.

kershaw

At BJ's, Sarah hands Faye a twelve-ounce cup of French Roast. She's wearing a Pink Floyd T-shirt today, and when she smiles her guileless smile she reminds Faye of Jen.

So how long will you be housesitting?

Till the end of summer.

And this friend you're watching the house for, what is he, a snowbird?

A what?

A snowbird. You know, one of those retirees who spends his summers up north?

Faye laughs, picturing Dieter in plaid shorts playing shuffleboard. No, no, he's not retired. He's my age!

Sarah moves over to the sink to rinse out a pair of demitasse cups. Setting the cups on a strainer, she glances over her shoulder.

So's this guy rich or what? Independently wealthy?

Not that either. He's a writer. I guess he can work anywhere he wants.

Sarah wipes her hands on a terrycloth towel. Then her brows crease in concentration: a writer? Wait a minute, she murmurs, this friend of yours, his name isn't Dieter is it?

Faye hesitates, unsure how much private information she should share. On the other hand, what would be the harm? Actually, she answers, it is.

Oh my God, I *love* his books! I read both of 'em! And he comes in here sometimes.

Does he?

Yeah, and he's really sweet. Sarah leans over the counter in confidence so the other customer in the shop, a studious young man with his nose deep inside a text book, won't overhear her. Really sweet, she whispers. And really fucking hot. 'Scuse my French.

No worries, Faye replies, shaking her head in amusement, I'm sure a lot of other women in this town agree with you. Anyway, Dieter'll be glad to hear that.

Hear what?

That you think he's hot.

Sarah's eyes grow as wide as a china doll's. She doesn't realize that Faye is pulling her leg. You wouldn't really do that, would you? Tell him that?

I'm kidding! 'Course I wouldn't.

I'd be *so* embarrassed.

No worries, hon, we'll keep it to ourselves. Dieter's got a big enough ego as it is.

As Faye approached Nirvana, the head shop down the block from the bakery, a middle-aged man stepped out of the store and squinted up at the glary white sky. In his button-down dress shirt and yellow power tie, he looked out of place next to Nirvana's haphazard window display of albums by Jefferson Airplane, psychedelic posters of Allen Ginsberg and Andy Warhol, and a cluster of hookahs and bongs. Spotting the yellow Lab, he crouched down on the sidewalk. Hey Sunny, he crooned. Hey there girl.

Faye allowed the dog enough leash for the man to scratch her ears and tousle her fur before he straightened back up with a crooked grin. Jet-black hair, thin sideburns, square jaw. Good looking, she thought distractedly. Takes care of himself.

Dave Kershaw, he announced, extending his hand.

Tentatively, Faye shook the man's hand. She wasn't comfortable confiding her name to a stranger so she nodded at Sunny instead.

Looks like you two know each other.

You bet we do, me and this girl go way back. He leaned down to tousle the dog's fur again then returned his attention to Faye. The length of his silent, probing gaze unnerved her.

So you must be Faye, he finally said. Faye Lindstrom.

In a dark corner of her mind a danger signal blinked on. She struggled to keep her voice from wavering.

How do you know that? How do you know my name?

He flashed his crooked smile, which now that she studied it more closely, looked like a smirk. A smirk that might hide a streak of disdain. Or something worse.

Well I'll tell ya, young lady, town like Crook? Ain't too many secrets in a town like this.

She didn't care for *young lady*. Didn't care for it one bit. Since he couldn't have been more than a few years older than her, it sounded condescending.

So what are you saying, that everyone in town knows my name?

No, I'm not saying that. I'm just saying that *I* do.

I see.

Do you?

Faye wasn't sure how to respond—*do you* sounded distinctly confrontational—so she decided to cut the conversation, the encounter, whatever this was, short. It was nice meeting you, Mr. Kershaw, she lied. She tugged at the dog's leash. C'mon Sunny, time to go.

Hey, wait a minute.

Sorry, Faye shrugged, I gotta go. Things to do.

But as she started to leave, Kershaw held up a hand to stop her. She didn't like that either.

Hold on a second. You *are* the one housesitting for Dieter, right?

Now, she thought, at least two people in town know. Do others? Grudgingly, she nodded.

Well I'm glad we bumped into each other then.

She tried to slow her breathing, to maintain composure. But the danger signal was blinking faster now.

Why's that?

'Cause I been meaning to stop by and see how you're doin'. See if you got settled in.

She didn't want to overreact and lash out at the man, or say something she might later regret, but her discomfort had turned into dismay, her dismay into anger. The nerve of this guy!

Look, I appreciate your concern, if that's what this is, but I don't need anyone to check up on me, okay?

Kershaw raised both hands this time.

That's not what I meant. What I meant—

What you meant, Faye cut in, or at least what you implied, is that I need someone to look after me, to check up on me. Which couldn't be further from the truth. Believe it or not, I'm perfectly capable of taking care of myself.

She yanked a little harder than she meant to on Sunny's leash, causing the Lab to whimper. She was boiling now. After Mexico, after Mestival, she had promised herself that she would never allow a man to dominate her again. Never allow a man like this, whoever he was, even a glimpse of weakness or self-doubt. Not after what she'd been through.

Hold on a second.

No, you hold on a second, Mr. Kershaw. If I was a guy housesitting for Dieter, would you stop by and see how *he* was doin'? Would you make sure *he* got settled in?

Kershaw looked a little stunned. But amused too. Tough, she thought. Resilient. Not easily offended.

Look, I gotta go, she repeated.

Fine, but listen . . . Frowning, he followed her for a few paces then gave up. He raised his voice, speaking to her back.

I think we got off on the wrong foot, Miss Lindstrom. Maybe if . . .

Refusing to respond, Faye yanked Sunny's leash again and strode purposefully away.

faye

She vowed not to let the encounter with Dave Kershaw bother her even though she knew that eventually she would second guess her behavior, obsess about what happened, and replay the scene over and over in her troubled mind.

Stay busy, keep moving, don't think.

She took a chicken breast out of the freezer for dinner. Checked the romaine lettuce to make sure it was still fresh. Then went out to the garden patch where Maggie grew her tomatoes to see if there were any left on the vines, only to discover that the remaining tomatoes were mostly pulp now, the vines tangled and overgrown from inattention.

She considered calling Dieter and asking him about Dave Kershaw, but she was afraid she might sound rash. Or unstable. It's a small town, she thought, word gets around, the man ran into Dieter last week, who happened to mention that an old friend was going to be watching his house . . . It was plausible, she supposed. But why would Dieter tell Kershaw my name? And why would Kershaw announce that he had been meaning to stop by?

She crossed the lawn to the tool shed, which was unlocked, and peeked inside. On the dusty shelves there was a spray bottle of weed killer and a rusty caulking gun. A pair of gloves, a pair of clippers. In a murky corner of the shed, a power saw perched on top of a leaf blower. Chisels, screwdrivers, putty knives dangling from hooks. Paint brushes. A stepladder. In her mind, a plan formed.

Recalling the half dozen two-by-sixes she had seen lying on top of the ceiling joists, she flicked on the light in the garage. Yes, these would do, these would do just fine. She tugged on the work gloves and climbed up the rungs of the stepladder, visualizing the box garden she would build and the trellis that would support the new vines. But as she carried the two-by-sixes out to the backyard, she noticed the old gardener at the hacienda in Mexico standing next to the swimming pool.

These ghosts, her therapist in Terre Haute once said. You see them often?

Often enough.

And they're always the same ones? The same people? The same ghosts?

Pretty much.

So what do you do when this happens?

I go on about my business. I don't pay them any mind. If you ignore them, Faye shrugged, they lose heart.

She knew that she must have sounded crazy, and maybe she was. But she was right, too. She glanced across the yard again. Sunny was lounging in Zen serenity beneath the lemon tree. The water in the pool lay still as a mirror. And the old gardener was gone.

After stacking the two-by-sixes on a pair of plastic sawhorses, she went upstairs to change into her swimsuit. Then dove into the pool to do her daily laps. In Terre Haute her therapist had told her that two of the keys to emotional stability were exercise and diet, so every day she swam laps, walked Sunny down to the harbor, and practiced yoga. Drank moderately. Ate nutritious meals.

Flinging a towel over her shoulders, she poured a glass of sun tea and started in on the next chapter of *To Kill a Mockingbird*, the one where Atticus Finch defends a black man falsely accused of rape. But even though the trial was riveting, her focus kept shifting away. She recalled how Dave Kershaw had gazed, without flinching, into her eyes. *So you must be Faye, Faye Lindstrom.* When Atticus, heartbroken by his client's conviction, strides out of the courtroom, the black families in the balcony stand up to show their silent respect, and the image of a black man in the balcony removing his hat as Atticus passes by brought tears to her eyes. But the tears quickly dried when she remembered Kershaw calling her *young lady*. Who is he, dammit, and how does he know my name? She should have asked him those questions point blank, but the way he stared at her had made her feel helpless, the way she used to feel when Mestival switched on the klieg lights and the men in the masks shuffled into the room for the next horrific scene. A sudden breeze gusted across the patio and she shuddered, twice, closing the book. Now that she thought about it, didn't Kershaw speak with a slight accent? And didn't he look, well, kind of foreign, kind of Hispanic? She recalled his jet-black hair and narrow sideburns trimmed, at the bottom, at a sharp angle. Wasn't that the style these days in Mexico, too?

Her heart began to drum against the cage of her chest and she knew that she was teetering on the cliff of one of her anxiety attacks. *Don't do this. Don't panic. Don't overreact.* Gasping—all of a sudden she couldn't catch her breath—she picked up the phone and dialed Dieter.

She flips the chicken breast on the grill, noting with satisfaction the dark grid of char marks on the opposite side. Then she looks across the patio, pleased, organized, back in control. The salad prepared, the wine decanted, the tiki torches lit. And a few minutes left before dinner to do what she needs to do.

At the patio table she pours herself a glass of chardonnay, opens the box of stationery she brought with her to Florida to write letters home, and silently thanking Dieter for quelling her unfounded fears, begins to compose a letter of apology to Detective Dave Kershaw of the Crooked River police department. The man Dieter asked to stop by and leave his business card just in case she had any concerns during her stay. The man who attended school with Maggie and became good friends with Dieter when the writer fictionalized his character in his second book.

Good lord, Faye cried into the phone, Kershaw? I *knew* that name rang a bell. He's the guy that shot Colt!

Dieter laughed. Nothing seemed to amuse him more than these literary mind games. Actually, he said, as far as I know Dave Kershaw has never shot anyone in his life.

But what about—

Made it up.

So what about that scene, you know, when Colt—

Made it up.

You made it up?

Yep.

But why would you do that?

She pictures the phone cradled against his shoulder, that pirate smile.

Ummm . . . because I'm a novelist? And that's what novelists do?

dieter

Tropical heat. The buzz of a fly. A close, dark room. Close. Closed in. Dark. Claustrophobic.

Picking up his pen, Dieter recalls the opening lines of Sartre's *Troubled Sleep . . . An octopus? He pulled out his knife and opened his eyes, it was a dream. No, it wasn't.*

Angelina wakes in a close, dark room unsure where she is or whether that really matters. Climbs out of bed, crosses the floor, and eases open a pair of wooden shutters painted the color of old denim, faded blue. Some of the paint has flaked off the slats and as she brushes the scales with her bare foot, an image of a man doing something awful to her the night before slides through her mind.

It was a dream. No, it wasn't.

Blue shutters, blue hills, a belt of gum trees. Flat savanna. Broiling sun. And of course the hacienda. In memory the rooms were cooler than this but perhaps she was last here in what passes, in Mexico, for winter.

He puts down his pen and refocuses on the unadorned study where he writes. Desk and a chair, futon where he sometimes naps when the words dry up. The walls are bare, the furnishings spartan except for an elaborate throw rug, a detailed representation of a tropical garden he brought home from Mexico the year he returned to Bloomington with Jen.

*

Angelina wakes, flings open the blue shutters, and sees a savanna flat as the winter cornfields of her childhood stretching away from a hacienda darkened by the shadows of calabash trees, the hacienda where the nightmare started; and where, perhaps, it must end.

A soft knock then Sanchez, the bodyguard with the gentle demeanor and mournful grey eyes, steps into the room carrying a breakfast tray. She isn't really hungry—she rarely is these days—and after a few bites of a warm tortilla she pushes the tray away. Only the black coffee, strong and potent, is savored.

The first sip jogs her out of a mental fog and kindles a brief spark of optimism. Maybe today there will be no filming. Maybe today Mestival will let her rest. The bodyguard lifts the tray, inquiring in broken English if she would like anything else.

More coffee, *por favor*.

With a courtly nod he leaves the room and returns a few minutes later with a second cup. The straw hat he's wearing looks out of place, it doesn't jibe with his holstered gun.

Gracias, she murmurs. *De nada*, he replies.

The other bodyguards project coiled violence—given the chance she's certain they would harm her—but Sanchez is different. Not for the first time she senses the embarrassment he feels for the things Mestival makes her do.

Dieter floats, daydreams, stares out the window at the unruly Indiana meadow he cuts down once a year with an old-fashioned scythe, his deltoids loosening with every swish of the blade, a sound that always reminds him—a writer can't help it—of the *chuck chuck chuck* of Cash Budren's adze in *As I Lay Dying*.

After breakfast Sanchez takes her out for their usual morning walk in the low hills that circle the savanna. His gait is loose and easy, and even though he has little to say this morning, the seed that was planted a few weeks ago when he turned away from her in modesty as she was getting dressed blossoms once again, a tiny flower of hope. If she's bold enough to propose such an outrageous idea, would he help her escape? The possibility is exhilarating, but what if she's mistaken? What if his deference is merely part of his job? What if he's just as loyal to Pablo Mestival as all the rest of them?

It's like receiving a sacrament, an unholy sacrament, the way the bodyguard delivers the hypodermic on a small silver tray. Every day Mestival, or one of his associates, calculates the dosage down to the final drop and personally cuts and cooks the exact amount of smack he wants her to inject. It's a fine science, a changeable arithmetic, the geometry of junk.

She taps the inside of her arm to wake the vein then slides the needle in while Sanchez, in apparent distress, turns away to stare out the window at the distant belt of gum trees losing their definition in the last seven minutes of light.

The initial jolt before she freefalls, muscles collapsing, into a dark canyon, deep space. Then a wave of sudden heat neutralizes the skin chills as she opens her eyes and sees the empty needle lying on the tray and the bodyguard on the hardback chair solemnly watching her. She asks for a glass of *agua*. Nodding, Sanchez moves toward the sink.

The pen lies on the page, the page on the desk. The writer paces the floor. He feels like a vulture circling a kill, circling Angelina the way he keeps circling, year after year, book after book, a small cadre of expats lifting shot glasses of mescal to the wonder of the world as the waves crawl up the Yucatan sands and the wind clicks in the palm fronds and someone picks up a guitar and strums the opening chords of a song they all know. Emboldened by drink, Dieter mouths the words of the familiar chorus while the others glance over at him with affection. Soon another voice joins in, then another, then more, creating a choir, a shared narrative, the story of their lives.

mr. gold

Henry Gold was not the type of man to judge strangers solely on the way they chose to dress. And yet as someone who in his four decades as general manager of the Gibson Hotel had welcomed thousands of guests to his esteemed establishment, he long ago determined that a refined taste in sartorial fashion tended to indicate good breeding, steadfast character, and a stable moral foundation. Just as poor taste often signaled the opposite. Of course over time, as fashions changed, Mr. Gold had been forced to take into account the fickle nature of trends. In the sixties and seventies, for instance, a young man sporting ragged cutoff jeans and one of those ludicrous tie dyed T-shirts raised the distinct (not to mention worrisome) possibility of a raucous party that evening in room 217. Because hippies, Mr. Gold had discovered, liked to gather in tribes willing to share whatever bounty they carried with them on their aimless journeys across America. A packet of marijuana. A pint of cheap booze. A new cassette tape by Crosby, Stills and Nash, or one of those other long-haired bands, Led Zeppelin. And yet nowadays a young woman who favored garish peasant blouses or bell-bottom blue jeans might well be the vice president of a branch bank in Toledo. Or she might be on the lam. It was getting harder and harder to tell.

Fortunately the other end of the fashion spectrum remained much easier to parse. Whenever an elderly couple strolled into the Gibson's ornate lobby wearing the kind of old-world finery that dominated *his* clothes closet too, Mr. Gold's spirits invariably brightened. For the gentleman a herringbone suit coat, or if it was August, a navy blue dress shirt tucked neatly inside grey slacks divided, in the front, by creases as sharp as knives. A little starch in the collar, a checkered ascot, perhaps a fob watch dangling from the inner pocket of a three-button vest? As for his lovely companion—oh how Mr. Gold cherished the aura of a well-heeled matron—an elegant but subdued evening gown accompanied by a slender string of black pearls and a jaunty white plume hat combined a sense of decorum with the whimsical nature befitting a woman who, in modern parlance, was *comfortable in her own skin*. Sadly, with so many malcontents bemoaning the fate of the white egrets slaughtered en masse to provide those lovely feathers, you rarely saw plume hats any more. And while Mr. Gold appreciated just as much as the next fellow an occasional glimpse of an egret or heron gliding across the salt flats on the outskirts of town, in his opinion the absence of such sartorial finery was merely one more reminder of misplaced political passion. First mink stoles. And now plume hats!

Still, whenever one of those distinguished older couples strolled into the Gibson, his expectations markedly rose. For more often than not these were the types of guests who would linger in the lobby after they had dressed for their evening out, politely requesting Mr. Gold's culinary recommendations while offering, in response, a few nuggets of insight into their personal affairs. Or better yet, urging Mr. Gold to cast a few of his own personal nuggets their way. For there was nothing the genteel manager liked better than to entertain strangers with the well-rehearsed sketch of his life here in Crooked River. What pleasure it gave him to describe his saintly mother, his steady, stoic father, and his dear, departed wife Virginia whose lovely face filled like a blossom the photo frame Mr. Gold had recently hung on the wall behind the front counter in the hope, he wasn't ashamed to admit, that a guest would inquire just who that splendid creature might be.

Unfortunately refined, well-bred guests were becoming a rarity these days, roundly replaced by a less civil, less courteous, less cultivated breed of customer. Such as the young man now leaning over the counter to sign the register. Once in a while the manager's initial misgivings about a new patron turned out to be wrong (how could he forget, for instance, his first inaccurate impression of William Dieter?), and he was more than willing under those circumstances to admit his mistake. But this time Mr. Gold doubted that his suspicions were unfounded. Slovenly dress (in this case, a pair of plaid shorts two sizes too large for the young man's slender frame topped by an outlandish green T-shirt featuring a cartoon duck) was one thing; a stringy, unwashed mop of black hair clearly revealing a tangle of blond roots quite another. Why, the manager couldn't help but wonder, would a handsome young man like this do such a thing to his hair? It was the worst dye job Mr. Gold had ever seen. And he had seen some real doozies.

faye

At a garden center out by the honey farms south of town, Faye picked up two ten-pound bags of fill dirt, a five-pound bag of steer manure, and half a dozen tomato plants. Before leaving the store, a display of brightly colored spiral trellises caught her eye, so she purchased six of those too. Then she stopped at BJ's to buy some pastries, her gaze roaming over the glittering glass shelves of apple strudel, chocolate truffles, and key lime pie.

So whatdya think, Sarah asked.

I think there's too many choices!

Tell me about it.

Faye pointed at one of the trays.

Are those fruit tarts?

Yep. With pastry cream.

Sounds good. Why don't you give me a dozen of those. And could you wrap 'em up in a box, please?

At the house she slipped on an old pair of khaki shorts and a faded denim work shirt and went outside to finish the box garden, cutting the two-by-sixes to length then clinching the corners with 16-penny nails. Placing the frame on top of two layers of landscape mesh, she poured fill dirt into the empty box before broadcasting half the bag of steer manure across the bed. With a hand spade she opened up holes for the tomato plants, which she carefully wedged out of their plastic containers. Then she cranked on the garden hose, topped the six small cavities with water and another sprinkle of steer manure, and finally secured a spiral trellis around each plant.

Upstairs she took a shower then lingered for a few minutes in front of the open closet trying to decide what to wear. Now that she had kicked her junk habit and her natural skin color had returned, her figure had fleshed back out to what it was before Mestival hooked her on dope. But she had to be careful not to overdo it. To look presentable but not flashy, attractive but down to earth. Above all she didn't want to give Dave Kershaw the wrong impression. It was imperative that she apologize for her behavior the other day, but she wasn't looking for a date.

Still, why not put your best face forward? In retrospect, her stubborn vow to forego makeup in Crooked River now seemed overly dramatic. What was the harm in a little eye shadow? Besides, if she had really meant to honor that vow she wouldn't have brought the kit with her in the first place. In the bathroom, she gazed into the mirror, recalling something her therapist in Terre Haute had said. It's *your* life now, Faye, no one else's. Do what *you* think's best.

Is Detective Kershaw in?

Betty, the dour, overweight, middle-aged woman straddling a stool behind the counter in the lobby of the police station regarded Faye without a hint of welcome. Then her gaze shifted to the cardboard box.

Would you mind setting that down here, she said, tapping the front counter.

The precinct was housed in an old brick building just off the central plaza. Through tall, narrow windows in the exterior wall of the lobby, streams of afternoon light poured across the terrazzo floor.

Although Faye didn't care for the woman's sour attitude, she obediently placed the box of fruit tarts on the counter.

Now would you mind, Betty instructed, telling me what's inside?

Tarts, Faye replied tartly.

Tarts?

Fruit tarts.

The dispatcher, or whatever her job title was, nodded.

For Detective Kershaw.

Excuse me?

The fruit tarts. They're for Detective Kershaw?

Matter of fact they are.

Maybe, Faye thought, this wasn't such a hot idea after all. Maybe I should just leave the tarts and the letter of apology and go home.

Look ma'am, is he in or not?

With an exaggerated sigh Betty flipped open the ledger on the counter and picked up a pen. Then she glanced up at a wall clock and jotted down the time.

Your name, please?

Excuse me?

Your name, Betty repeated in a flat tone. I need your name.

But why is *that* important?

In slow motion, Betty raised her head and froze Faye with a dead stare.

Fine. Faye. My name's Faye Lindstrom.

Okay then. Please take a seat on the bench over there, Faye Lindstrom, and I'll see if Detective Kershaw's available.

A few minutes later Kershaw strode across the lobby smiling his lopsided smile. As she stood up, he extended his hand.

Faye! It's good to see you. Is it all right to call you that by the way? Faye?

Of course. And it's good to see you too.

For a few moments an awkward silence filled the room. Behind the counter, Betty watched her closely, gauging her every move.

So what can I do for you, Faye?

She paused, gathering her thoughts. It had been so much easier to say these things on paper. So I was thinking about the other day, she finally responded. You know, in front of Nirvana?

Kershaw waited for her to continue but she seemed to have lost track of what she was going to say. Noting how she kept glancing across the lobby, clearly discomforted by Betty's insistent scrutiny, he reached out and cupped her elbow and lowered his voice. Maybe we should talk about this in private.

Faye looked baffled, as if shocked by his suggestion.

In private?

In my office. I think you might be more comfortable there.

Kershaw punched a code into an electronic keypad next to a set of double doors, and when the doors sighed open Faye grabbed the fruit tarts off the front counter and followed him inside.

The second room was larger than the lobby but staler too, and windowless. Four bulky oak desks, all but one unoccupied. A water cooler. File cabinets. A map of the Florida panhandle tacked to one of the walls. It looked like a movie set from the fifties, as if at any moment Frank Sinatra or Lee J. Cobb might wander out of a back office clutching a sheaf of papers.

Like the precinct room, Kershaw's office was windowless and musty. The overhead light illuminated institutional green walls and a desk cluttered with files. A black telephone. A stained mug.

Can I get you something? Coffee? Iced tea?

No, nothing, I'm fine.

Okay then. Please. He indicated a chair on the opposite side of the desk. Have a seat.

Before sitting down she placed the box of pastries on the desk. Then she leaned the sealed letter against it.

After hesitating for a few moments, staring at the cardboard box with pursed lips, as if he feared it might contain a small bomb, Kershaw reached out, put the letter aside, and lifted the lid. Well now, what a pleasant surprise, he exclaimed, ogling the fruit tarts. Thank you.

It's the least I could do.

For what?

Faye paused, wondering why she was so nervous.

For being so rude the other day. That's why I came here, to apologize for being rude. The thing is, I didn't know who you were.

Kershaw let the box lid close and leaned back in his chair, folding his hands.

But you do now.

I called Dieter.

Did you?

I did. And he told me . . . you know.

No, actually, I don't. Told you what?

His succinct manner—all these direct, detective-like questions that didn't sound like questions—was a little unsettling, but she wasn't going to let Kershaw sense her anxiety. That you were a detective, she replied in a sober voice. That you were a detective and a friend and that he asked you to stop by the house and check up on me.

Kershaw trained his dark-eyed gaze on her again and she didn't know whether to feel flattered or afraid. It's the same look he must give two-bit criminals, she thought. Nickel baggers, petty thieves, guys who beat up their wives. Then his gaze abruptly softened and he clapped and rubbed his hands, as if he had just cracked a difficult case. Okay then, he cried. Apology accepted!

He was rooting through the box of tarts now. And when he glanced up at her she was surprised by his shy, furtive expression, like a boy caught with his hand in the proverbial cookie jar.

You mind if I try one of these?

Actually, she responded, I do.

This time the detective was the one at a loss for words. Taken aback. Befuddled.

You do?

I do . . . Unless, she added coyly, I can have one too.

She was pleased by his obvious relief. Pleased even more by the realization that she still knew how to flirt. God, how long has it been since I flirted?

Grinning his crooked grin, Kershaw held the box out for her.

You first, he said.

*

As the sun slipped behind the palms on Christopher Key, the light glancing off the shrimp trawlers in the marina began to pearl, to grey. Straining against her leash, Sunny trotted down the old wooden planks between rows of boats inside their moorings. Some of the slips were empty, and as the wind freshened off the Gulf, whitecaps rolled across the harbor and sloshed against the exposed pilings. Soon the moon, almost full tonight, would raise its orange fist over the water and glow down on the hulls of the trawlers, the oyster boats, the *Patti Belle*.

At the end of the boardwalk Faye circled back toward town, crossing through the working-class neighborhood where many of the deckhands lived. Her heart weighed a little heavy as she considered the hardscrabble front yards, the patchy grass and rusty swing-sets, the plastic chairs. Red and white buoys dangling from fence posts. Horseshoe pits. She tried to imagine what it would be like to live here, this close to the boats you labored on day after day.

The light was falling fast now as Sunny dragged her past the police station. Earlier, in Kershaw's office, after finishing a second fruit tart, Faye had stood up. The detective had risen too.

I'll walk you out to your car.

But I didn't drive, she said, playing coy again.

Then I'll walk you out to the sidewalk, he parried.

They paused in front of the precinct. She had the impression that Kershaw wanted to say something besides goodbye but wasn't quite sure how to go about it. Her skin tingled with anticipation.

You like boats, Faye?

He was trying to sound casual but she suspected that he was just as nervous as she was. Sure, she answered. I mean I haven't spent a lot of time on them, but sure.

What about fishing. You like to fish?

In her mind she once again trolled out to the salt flats of Ascension Bay with Dieter to fly cast for bonefish. Spotting the silver fish in the watery glare then judging their speed through the shallows, she practiced casting her line in their path. Sometimes they struck. Sometimes they didn't. I do, she answered. When we were kids my dad used to take me and my sister out to the lakes around Terre Haute. And I did a little fishing in Mexico too. Bonefishing. With Dieter.

She warned herself to be careful. Kershaw projected the kind of self-confidence you would expect in a police detective but she had already witnessed flashes of vulnerability too. She didn't want to be too direct and scare him away.

Why?

Why?

No, I mean I was just wondering why you asked.

He hesitated, choosing his words. The thing is I live on this lake, he eventually replied. Lake Baylor? And I keep a boat out there, a pontoon boat. He looked up at the sky, stretching the muscles in his neck, presumably easing a knot of tension.

Say it, she thought, suddenly anxious. Just go ahead and say it.

Anyway, I thought you might like to come out some day. Toss in a line.

She let out a breath, almost groaning with relief. Well thank you, sir. That sounds fun. I'll think about it, okay?

You could bring Sunny, he added, upping the ante.

I'm sure she'd like that. She seems very fond of you.

The crooked grin then the dark-eyed gaze followed, once again, by a softening. He clapped and rubbed his hands, cracking another case.

Okay then! All righty! Reaching into his shirt pocket, he handed her his card.

chance

The night he checked into the Gibson, Chance slept like a lamb, his body catching up on the rest it so desperately needed now that his bout with food poisoning at the motel from hell was safely behind him. Fully energized, he hopped out of bed the next morning and took a long hot shower, disappointed but not particularly surprised by the lack of water pressure in the pipes. For what an old-school warhorse like the Gibson lacked in modern creature comforts—no Swedish mattresses here!—was effectively countered by its undeniable charm. Toweling off, he regarded the room. A tasteful seascape—a pair of winged trawlers anchored in Crooked River's picturesque harbor—painted, according to a small sign underneath it, by a local artist. A blue cloud of a comforter floating on top of the bed. In lieu of a closet a mahogany armoire. Situated on the Gibson's top floor, the room's double window featured a sweeping view of the downtown plaza, the wheel of streets that fanned out from it, and in the distance, Christopher Key.

He was ravenous. What he wanted, what he craved this morning was bacon and eggs, pecan pancakes, a cinnamon roll. Out the window he saw the sign for the Delta Café and had to remind himself to remain cautious. The previous evening he had looked up Dieter's name in the city directory and discovered not just the phone number but his address too, on Magnolia Street. Spreading a map of the town on top of the bed, he'd located the neighborhood mere blocks from the hotel, which meant that he had to be careful not to expose himself. The Delta Café would no doubt meet his needs, but for all he knew Faye and Dieter might choose to dine there this morning also.

He drove north along a coastal road separating an orderly corridor of inland pines from rocky beaches, briny mud flats, and occasional vistas of the pewter-grey sea. Though they remained invisible in the morning fog rolling in off the water, every few minutes he heard the whine of a Navy jet streaking along the coast on maneuvers, the pilots in the clouds dependent on their instruments. Clicking on his high beams to pierce the mist, he cruised through a dreamlike landscape. Tendrils of fog wrapped like whips around watery pilings. Houses on stilts marching, in lockstep, toward Apalachicola Bay.

As the fog began to lift, he spotted a roadside diner overlooking a brackish stream. Inside, he chose a table next to a screened window with a view of the tannic river, a towering live oak tree, and a solitary jon boat roped to a rickety dock. After a quick scan of the menu, he listened to a pair of bullfrogs croak back and forth on the muddy bank, checked out the waitress's legs, then consumed, without hesitation, his bacon and eggs, Belgian waffle dripping with maple syrup, coffee black as tar. He liked the diner because it was peaceful there, the food was good, and the other customers ignored him. But he was feeling out of sorts, too, his initial burst of energy that morning tempered by troubling thoughts. Ordering a second cup of coffee, he noticed half a dozen white egrets perched like the petals of an elaborate carnation in the mossy arms of the live oak, but even this bewitching sight did not really soothe him. Because the moral implications of what he was about to do now that he had arrived in Florida had dampened his spirits. The darkness was closing in.

Ever since his late teens—ever since his years in Eugene and his initial sojourns to Mexico—he had suffered periodic episodes of melancholia, freefalling into the gloom of despair, and he was afraid that he was teetering on that precipice once again. The signals were all too familiar. Shortness of breath. Sudden fatigue. A pervasive sense of dread and hopelessness. As he cruised back south on the coastal highway he tried to enjoy the beautiful views—the sun had finally come out and those sudden glimpses of the sea were spectacular now—but just as he had feared, the old sadness had gripped its talons around his heart and wasn't about to let go.

For the next two days, he mostly stayed in his room. Pacing the floor. Scanning the pages of the Tallahassee Democrat with little interest or comprehension. Watching daytime TV. On the second morning, during a brisk walk through a working-class neighborhood off the central square, he stopped at a convenience store for the daily paper, a loaf of bread, and a jar of peanut butter, determined to hole up in the Gibson until the battle was over. In the steely grip of melancholia, it was wise to avoid people, your haggard reflection in a shop window, or the sun hammering down on the pavements. Idle chatter sounded like gunshots, hard light blurred vision, paranoia ran amok.

Back in his room he popped a Xanax and fell asleep and dreamed phantasmagoria: sacrificial altars, vultures tearing apart a carcass, his grandfather's grave. Waking in a deep funk, he sat groggily by the window watching the good citizens of Crooked River go about their business on the streets below.

It would be so easy to give up. He looked over at the duffel lying on the floor. The handgun was under the clothes. All he had to do was insert the barrel in his mouth, kiss the world goodbye, and pull the trigger. Or choose a more dramatic route, leap out the window with a rebel yell, his final moments punctuated by the startled faces of Crooked River shoppers gazing up in astonishment at the man falling through the air.

He felt as ill as he had in Georgia though he knew that this time the symptoms were all in his mind, in his sick mind. Turning away from the open window, he fled the toxic room. Outside the sun was scorching the pavements like a laser beam. He circled left, ignoring the faces, the voices, a car horn, keeping his eyes on the sidewalks until he came to a curb and discovered that he was in an older residential neighborhood now. Antebellum houses, expensive German cars, manicured lawns green and cool in the shade of gnarled mimosas. Some of the roots of the trees had cracked the sidewalk and twice he stubbed his toes, yelping in pain and cursing his clumsiness. He needed to go back to his room. For a day, two, however long it took. At the next intersection he wheeled right, quick-marched one more block and spun to the right again, retracing his steps back to the square. Then he glanced up at the street sign and noted, to his horror, that he was traversing Magnolia, the street where Dieter lived. He quickened his pace, his heart thudding, his palms damp, the anxiety inside him as black and destructive as the funnel of a tornado scattering, to eternity, the remnants of a town.

That night he took another Xanax, chased it with a can of Budweiser, and vowed, as he had vowed so many times before, that he wouldn't give in to despair. He closed the window to remove temptation. Left the handgun in the duffle. And somehow, for the next few hours, kept his inner demons at bay.

And when he woke the next morning, his melancholia had disappeared. In his sleep, the demons had dissolved. With a renewed sense of purpose, he brushed his teeth. Combed his hair. Strung open the blinds on the harbor in the distance gleaming like a sheet of silver in the sun.

mr. gold

Hearing a thump of footsteps, Mr. Gold glanced up from the hotel register, surprised to see Chance bounding down the stairway. For the past two days, the Gibson's latest eccentric guest had hardly left his room.

Well now, young man, aren't we looking chipper today!

Chance gave Mr. Gold a playful salute. The hotel manager was an odd duck all right—what was up, for instance, with those red bow ties?—but you couldn't deny his cordiality.

Chipper indeed, sir.

If you don't mind my saying so, you looked a bit under the weather yesterday. But you're better now, I presume?

Oh yes, much better. Much better! To Mr. Gold's delight Chance arched his arms over his head like Zorba the Greek and performed a few steps of the traditional folk dance *sirtaki*.

Yes well, in my four decades in the hospitality business, Mr. Gold effused, and let me just add what a wonderful four decades they've been, I've noticed that travel can be hard on a man. We're creatures of habit, as I'm sure you know, and travel robs us of those habits. And sometimes our immune systems rebel.

Chance was staring out the Gibson's front windows. As a reward for surviving his latest bout of melancholia, he planned to treat himself to a day at the beach. Preoccupied with visions of body surfing, blondes in red bikinis, and an ice-cold bottle of beer, he failed to register the manager's next question.

Excuse me?

The reason for your visit. I couldn't recall if we've already discussed this. Business, is it?

Reminding himself to remain polite, and thus avoid suspicion, Chance replied, with a lecherous smirk, well, not *just* business.

Ah yes, Mr. Gold murmured, vaguely offended (but determined not to show it) by the young man's tasteless remark. But then again *your* business, he exclaimed, is really none of my own. You must forgive me for being so inquisitive.

That's quite all right, sir, I have nothing to hide.

Of course you don't, Mr. Gold practically shouted, staring with suspicion at the man's blond roots.

Actually, Chance confided, I'm on my way to the Keys. On assignment. He was improvising now, winging it. What the hell, he thought, if the old codger gets off on stuff like this, why not play along? He darted furtive glances around the Gibson's ornate lobby, as if he suspected that a foreign agent might be lurking behind one of the potted palms. I'm in surveillance you know, he whispered.

Surveillance! At first Mr. Gold appeared startled, then impressed. My goodness. All sort of hush hush, I take it? That kind of work?

Yes indeed, *very* hush hush. But let me tell ya, it's been some kinda interesting life.

Well I certainly have no doubt about *that*!

So interesting, in fact, that I've decided to write my memoirs. I mean not yet, at my age and all. But one day.

Of course.

And to be honest, that's the real reason I stopped here. In your little town. 'Cause I've been doing a lot of reading lately.

Naturally.

You know, research.

Ah yes, tradecraft, the manager ventured, recalling a word from an old spy flick.

And I found out, Chance expounded, that one of my favorite writers lives right here, right here in Crooked River.

Mr. Gold could not have been more pleased. He silently congratulated himself for steering the conversation in this particular direction. I assume, he winked, that you're referring to one William Dieter?

Indeed I am.

Well, young man, you are hardly the first literary type to venture down to our fair town hoping to catch a glimpse of our esteemed local writer.

I'm not surprised.

Why just the other day matter of fact—

'Course I would never impose on the man, Chance assured him. That wouldn't be right. Besides, if I did happen to meet him, I'd probably be tongue-tied, star-struck, you know?

Understandable. But you really wouldn't have to worry about that.

I wouldn't?

Not at all. Trust me, despite his well-earned acclaim, our resident scribe remains as down to earth as anyone I know. There isn't an arrogant bone in the man's body.

Well who knows then, Chance replied with a false smile, maybe I'll get lucky and run into him after all. You think he'd mind if I asked for an autograph? I have his new book with me you know. You think he'd sign it?

Mr. Gold adjusted his bow tie; in the summer heat the knots sometimes loosened. I'm sure Mr. Dieter would be more than happy to sign your book, he guaranteed his guest. But I'm afraid he won't be able to.

Oh? Why not?

Because Mr. Dieter and his lovely wife Maggie spend their summers up north now. They've turned into a couple regular snowbirds. And who, pray tell, can blame them?

They're not here?

They're not here.

Chance's heart sank. If Dieter wasn't there then neither was Faye. That's too bad, he muttered despondently, staring off into space. He felt a sharp stab of anxiety, then a surge of panic. What now? His plans were shot, his prospects non-existent. Maybe I'll just drive by and take a picture of his house instead, he shrugged. Guess there'd be no harm in taking a photo of an empty house.

Later Mr. Gold would scold himself for being such a blabbermouth. But how could he have known what was going to happen? Well, not exactly empty, he said.

Sir?

The house, Mr. Gold repeated, isn't exactly empty. Someone's housesitting for the summer. A young woman, I've been told.

A young woman?

An old friend. Someone, I believe, he met down in Mexico.

Instantaneously Chance's despair turned into joy. The house-sitter had to be Faye. And that meant that she was all alone. Unprotected. Defenseless. What a stroke of blind luck! He couldn't have scripted the scenario any better if he wrote it himself.

On his way out the door, Chance turned back to the beaming manager. Catch ya later, Mr. Gold. Then he arched his hands over his head and once again performed the *sirtaki*, clicking his fingers to a swell of music only a Shaolin could hear.

Lureen

Well look at *you*, sugar. Why you're just as pretty as a peach, a little ole Georgia peach.

Startled, Faye took a step back as the woman in the outlandish white hat barged through the front door then leaned forward to offer, presumably for a kiss, her perfumed cheek. Not wishing to give offense, Faye dutifully pecked, and in turn the woman pecked back, kissing the air.

My sister told me you were a real looker, the woman gushed, but I wasn't prepared for *this*. You're a genuwine knockout, honey.

Your sister?

Maggie!

Oh my God, so you're Lureen?

Right here in the flesh, Lureen crowed, wiggling past her. Right here in the living flesh.

As they sipped iced tea out on the patio, Faye assured Lureen that everything was fine. She loved the house, she said, it was so peaceful and quiet there. She loved taking Sunny for walks down to the harbor, Crooked River was such an enchanting town. And she was keeping busy too, she added, pointing out the new tomato garden.

My goodness, you did all that by yourself?

I did.

Well I'm impressed. Personally I can't tell one end of a hammer from the other but hey, that's just me!

Without a hint of embarrassment Lureen tilted her head for a closer look at Faye's bare legs. I'll tell you one thing, honey, I better not let Charlie get a gander at those gams of yours. He might not be able to handle it. She winked, conspiratorially. His heart, you know.

Faye had to stifle a laugh. Gams? Did the woman really say gams?

After she finished her iced tea, Lureen scribbled her address and phone number on a note pad, tore the sheet off, and handed it to Faye. Then she stood up to leave.

So listen, sugar, if there's anything you need you just let me know, okay? Anything at all.

Actually, Faye said, I would like to ask you something.

Ask away.

Do you know Dave Kershaw?

Lureen hesitated, crinkling her eyes. Dave Kershaw? The detective?

Yeah, the detective.

Well now. Lureen's sudden grin looked decidedly lascivious. I see, she purred, sitting back down.

See what? Faye wondered.

An hour later, in Lureen's Chevy convertible, they crossed the causeway to Christopher Key. As the morning fog lifted and the sun peeked over the Gibson, the town's tallest building, and showered the harbor with streams of pale light, Faye leaned back against the leather upholstery, watching a pair of oyster boats follow the channel south, bound for the beds off Carrabelle. Having already grown accustomed to Lureen's seemingly boundless energy, that bizarre psychological fusion of high-pitched sexual fervor and unshakable ecclesiastical belief, she felt more relaxed in her manic company now, and she was looking forward to spending some time with her at the beach.

After a long, invigorating swim and a dozen games of fetch with Sunny, they slathered their arms and legs with sunscreen and talked about Dave Kershaw. Lureen sketched in the general background, describing how Kershaw's father, a former police officer in New Orleans, took an early retirement following some kind of traumatic incident in the French Quarter, resettling with his wife and their two kids in a condo overlooking Panama City Beach. And then how, less than a year later, baffled by her husband's withdrawal, the emotional shell he had crawled into when they left New Orleans, Kershaw's mother filed for divorce, and with the two kids in tow relocated to Crooked River.

Maggie and Kershaw became friends at Crooked River High, Lureen said, where they were in the same class. After graduation they stayed in touch, and when Dieter asked Maggie to marry him, she introduced the newly-promoted detective to her fiancé. Apparently recognizing in each other a kindred spirit, Dieter and Kershaw started hanging out together, fishing Lake Baylor or canoeing down the Blackwater River or watching baseball games on the television above the bar at The Tides. And when Dave's marriage began to founder (which, of course, is a whole *other* story, Lureen confided) Dieter helped guide his friend through those treacherous waters. After the divorce, he also filled some of the long hours of Dave's loneliness by inviting him to the house for a home-cooked meal or up to Tallahassee for a Florida State football game even though Maggie claimed that the real reason her husband courted the man's friendship was because he wanted to expand his cameo in *Fever Tree* into a major role in the next book, in the sequel. A Cajun cop? Are you kidding? He's probably *already* writing about him, Maggie exclaimed. But my sister, Lureen shrugged, always says stuff like that.

On the drive home from the beach they cruised past a blue Monte Carlo traveling in the opposite direction and for one wild, disorienting moment Faye could have sworn she recognized the driver. The high cheekbones, wraparound shades, pronounced chin cleft. But that wasn't possible. There was no way, she assured herself, that it could have been him. For one thing, the driver's hair was black. Chance was a blonde.

She lifted her face to the wind and let it blow away her worries. Another ghost, she decided, that's all it was. They seemed to be everywhere these days.

*

At the house, Faye thanked Lureen for the lovely outing and stood in the driveway waving as the convertible pulled away. Then she shuffled out to the patio and collapsed in a chair, exhausted. Lureen was sweet and charming and as genuwine as a southern belle could possibly be, but spending an afternoon with her was like spending a few hours in a hurricane; the woman's inner barometer, the shifting winds of her enthusiasm, rose and fell at a bewildering rate. Still, the day had not been wasted. For one, Lureen's insights into Dave Kershaw's private life—his rocky relationship with his troubled father and the disastrous, short-lived marriage—had given her an intriguing glimpse of the man behind the police badge.

She went upstairs and took a shower to wash the salt out of her hair. Hanging the wet towel on the hook on the back of the door, she thought about cooking dinner but changed her mind. She'd pick up a pizza instead. Or better yet, one of those muffaletta sandwiches Lureen kept raving about. Apparently the Cajun place was only a few blocks away.

At the beach, Lureen had looked her in the eye. That's the kind of thing you can let him know, she suggested.

Faye had no idea what the woman was talking about. Let him know?

When you go out to Lake Baylor. That's the kind of thing you can slip into the conversation, right? How much you love Cajun cooking?

But I haven't made up my mind yet, Faye protested.

Whether you like Cajun cooking? Are you crazy? Everyone likes Cajun cooking!

No, no, whether I'm going out there. To the lake. I haven't made up my mind yet.

Shocked, Lureen twisted her beach chair in the sand until she faced her companion head on.

Look, I don't mean to be bossy, hon, but let me tell you somethin', okay? In this town you ain't gonna find another Dave Kershaw. You're gonna find lowlifes and losers and guys steppin' out on their wives, sure. But you ain't gonna find another Dave Kershaw. I mean the dude's dreamy, right?

Right.

He's also single.

Uh huh.

And he's got a good job too! For cryin' out loud, girl, what else could you possibly want?

Faye thought about that for a moment.

A pontoon boat?

Lureen was so delighted with Faye's wry aside she reached out and squeezed both her hands. Well he's got one of those too, she bellowed. With those big ole cushions on it. You put those cushions down on the deck of that boat, honey, and you got yourself a bed!

kershaw

When the call came in to the precinct Betty patched it through to Kershaw, who cradled the phone against his shoulder while listening, with a resigned sigh, to Henry Gold drone on about the latest questionable (in his eyes that is) guest at the Gibson Hotel. Twice he nodded impatiently and tried to cut in but Mr. Gold's mellifluous voice wasn't about to allow an interruption. You had to let the manager wind down on his own.

At the end of the recitation, Kershaw finally managed to squeeze in a word or two. I understand, Henry . . . Yes, of course . . . Let's make it, what—the detective looked down at his wristwatch—around two?

For the rest of the morning, he went over old files, the inexplicable murder of little Jenny Thompson and the disappearance of the math teacher at Crooked River High, two recent cold cases that remained unsolved. Like the victims of the senseless crimes he dealt with every day, Kershaw yearned for closure in every case he was involved in but cold files were open wounds that continued to fester, that refused to heal, and there was always a kernel of self-doubt, a nagging suspicion that he might have missed something obvious during the initial investigation, something that even now could reignite the case and lead to its conclusion.

At noon Betty knocked on his door to ask if he wanted a sandwich from the drugstore. Or maybe a chocolate malt? Sure, he answered. Anything. Thanks.

*

A few minutes later Officer Patty Jones ambled into the precinct room, went over to one of the unoccupied desks, and placed a phone call. Spotting her through his open door, Kershaw waited for Patty to hang up the phone before he approached the desk, greeted her with his lopsided smile, and asked after her little girl, hoping to deflect their usual sexual banter. A few weeks ago at a party the two of them had overindulged in a bottle of Southern Comfort and ended up groping each other in the hostess's walk-in pantry before realizing just how reckless their behavior had become. Patty's husband, through one thin wall, wasn't ten feet away.

He asked her about Tommy Bouchard, the former Hell's Angel with the motorcycle repair shop east of town. Unbeknownst to his neighbors, Bouchard was living in Crooked River under federal protection. And according to the latest rumors, the chapter of the Angels he dropped a dime on in California may have tracked him down. He asked Patty if she thought they should move him.

Move him?

Yeah, move him.

Where?

I'm not sure. Haven't really thought about it. Maybe out by that strip club, the Black Kat.

Look, if you keep Bouchard in this town, anywhere in this town, anywhere *near* this town, how hard's it gonna be for those good old boys to find him? We're talkin' about Crooked River here, boss.

Kershaw grinned. Despite his misgivings, he liked the way she said *boss*. It sounded provocative. You're right, he conceded. I'll talk to Maguire about relocating him. South. Maybe Tampa.

Good, dude's a creep.

Oh yeah? I bet you say that about all the guys, he called over his shoulder.

All the guys but you, boss.

Betty came back from the drugstore with a chicken salad sandwich and a chocolate malt. While he ate, he scanned more files. A botched drug deal. An attempted rape. The guy on McKinley Drive who shot his next door neighbor's Chihuahua for barking in the middle of the night. The human comedy, he thought sourly. Every fucking day.

Pocketing his compact camera, he left the office, keenly aware of Patty Jones's unrelenting gaze tracking him across the room. Unless he was misreading her latest signals, which he seriously doubted, Patty would gladly drive out to Lake Baylor on a moment's notice and slide into his bed. But he had to steer clear of that. Screwing a married cop could prove disastrous. If someone, particularly Patty's husband, a contractor with an explosive temper and forearms like Virginia hams, found out, all hell would break loose. On his way across the precinct room an image of Faye Lindstrom flickered through his mind. Now *that* was a different kettle of fish. Faye was just as attractive as Patty, but she was also single and unattached and he hadn't stopped thinking about her since she came to his office the other day and presented him that box of pastries.

As he crossed the central square on his way to the Gibson, he thought about Faye down in Quintana Roo. Before asking Kershaw to check up on her, Dieter had described the entire sordid tale, from the early days of innocence in the village by the sea to her sexual debasement at the hands of strangers, in the unforgiving glare of klieg lights, at the hacienda west of Tulum. Nodding, Kershaw said he understood Dieter's concern and that he would be glad to help out.

To a hardened cop the story wasn't particularly shocking, but now that he had met the poor woman in the flesh it made him sad to recall it. So young, so vulnerable, so naïve when it all went down. A genuine hippie, Dieter called her, a flower child, the earth mother everyone in that village adored. Because unlike many of the other expats who had ventured down to the Yucatan to get high, Dieter said, or to get laid, or both, Angelina ("I mean Faye") actually believed in all that sixties' rainbow rhetoric. Peace and love. Spiritual balance. World harmony.

Like his father, he thought, she must suffer terribly, daily, the ordeal she miraculously survived. And yet *unlike* his father she seemed to be handling it remarkably well. The detective admired that. He had always been drawn to women who could take care of themselves, who were just as tough and resilient as he was, and there was no doubt in his mind that unlike his ex-wife, Faye Lindstrom fit that bill.

Thirty minutes later, leaving the Gibson, Kershaw strode across the street to a small parking lot reserved for guests of the hotel. He located the blue Monte Carlo, took out a notepad, and jotted down the numbers on the license plate. Then with his compact camera he snapped two photos, one from the back of the car and one from the side.

From his fourth-floor window Chance watched, in shock and dismay, as Kershaw retraced his steps across the lot. His heart was thumping so fiercely he feared it might burst. What the fuck was going on here? Who the hell *is* this guy and why's he taking photographs of my car? Focusing his binoculars on the parking lot, he memorized the man's features: black hair, chiseled face, sideburns cut at a sharp angle. He was a handsome dude. He dressed sharp as tacks. And he had cop written all over him.

Seated in the captain's chair of the pontoon boat cleated to his private dock, Kershaw flicks a line into the adjoining cove, hoping to coax another bass with the chartreuse jig skittering across the becalmed surface of Lake Baylor. When the wind weakens and the water lies down like this, the chartreuse jig, he's discovered, could be particularly effective.

With growing anticipation he considers Faye Lindstrom's upcoming visit. The adrenaline that streamed through his body when he answered the phone that afternoon and realized who it was had surprised him. In the back of his mind—in the back of every bachelor's mind, he supposes—he had been expecting rejection. Then the phone in his office rang and in a voice as bright as a beam of light

Faye said she'd given it some thought and yes, she'd like to come out to the lake and do some fishing. He suggested Sunday, and without hesitation she agreed.

On his way home from work, he had stopped at Winn-Dixie to pick up supplies. He wasn't sure what Faye liked to eat—he had forgotten to ask her—so he decided to cover the gamut. Brats and a bell pepper and sesame seed buns but also a package of those new meatless burgers in case she turned out to be a vegetarian. He didn't know much about hippies, but weren't a lot of them vegetarians? Beer and wine, or in case she didn't drink, sparkling soda. Striding down the produce aisle, he decided to make potato salad to go with the brats and grabbed a handful of spuds, a can of black olives, and two stalks of celery. Dill pickles. A jar of Dijon.

Sometimes in the late afternoon he puttered past the shelf to the other side of the lake to troll shiners for bass on the perimeter of the grass mats spread out like oil spills along the far bank. But more often, lately, he's been content to fish from the dock. Casting the jig into the center of the cove, he recalls fishing with his father, those boyhood excursions down on the Bayou Teche where they trolled the briny channel with crankbait for catfish and drum. It was a long time ago and he rarely even speaks to his dad these days, but still, those halcyon days on the waters of southern Louisiana remain anchors.

Like a patriarch hoisting a fishing rod instead of a scepter, he surveys his watery kingdom. Another pontoon boat patiently crosses the channel. From the crown of a loblolly pine, an osprey unfolds its wings and loops out over the water. On the far bank the setting sun casts a burnished glow on Vince Richardson's empty cabin. And now something strikes his line and he instinctively snaps the rod backwards and snags it: a smallmouth bass just over the legal limit. He unhooks the fish and places it in the well with the two others he has already caught. Later he'll coat the slender filets with corn meal and pan fry them in clarified butter for his supper. Either eat the fish or let it go, his father used to counsel. But never kill an animal for fun.

He reaches into a Coleman cooler next to the captain's chair and retrieves a can of beer. Popping the top, he replays the events of the day: the cold files that continue to nag him, Patty Jones's smoky grey eyes, Faye's unexpected phone call, and finally his surprising conversation with Henry Gold. The eccentric hotel manager tended to be overly imaginative, but this time around Kershaw has to admit that he might have latched on to something credible.

mr. gold

The first thing that had struck Mr. Gold about Chance, the manager reported, was his incredibly inept dye job. Why, he wanted to know, would a handsome young man like that do such a thing to a perfectly fine head of hair? Who was he trying to fool with such a disguise?

Standing on the opposite side of the front counter in the Gibson's ornate lobby, Kershaw nodded, feigning interest in what he suspected was nothing more than a red herring, a false alarm.

Then there was the guest's sudden announcement that he was *in surveillance*, Mr. Gold continued. Doesn't it seem odd, detective, that someone would blurt out his vocation to a virtual stranger even though he subsequently admitted that his line of work is, indeed, *hush hush*? And not just blurt it out, Mr. Gold added for emphasis, but downright brag about it, claiming that one day he was going to pen a memoir about his adventures?

Which brought up the manager's third point. Writers read, he said, as if Kershaw couldn't have figured that out for himself. That's what they do. They write. And they read. Why, when Dieter stayed here he must have had a dozen books in his room! But Chance? No sir, not a one. Not a single volume.

If you don't mind my asking, Kershaw interjected, how do you know this, Henry?

That writers read?

No, that he doesn't have any books in his room.

Because the housekeeper told me.

The housekeeper?

Right before she told me about the gun.

So this, Kershaw thought, is what it feels like to be manipulated. The hinge pivots, the door swings open, and the detective, on cue, steps through.

The gun? What kind of gun?

A Walther PPK .380 semi-automatic, Mr. Gold automatically replied. You know, the one with seven rounds?

Yeah, I know the gun, Henry. But wait. That's how she identified it?

Well . . .

What is she, a collector?

Actually, Mr. Gold confessed, Consuela wouldn't know a Magnum from a squirt gun.

I see, Kershaw murmured. And indeed he did. Saw Henry Gold sneaking around room 416 opening up dresser drawers, lifting the clothes in a duffel bag to peek underneath, snooping. You cased the joint, he said drolly.

A passionate fan of film noir, Mr. Gold was delighted by the quaint phrase. Cased the joint, he cried.

And found the gun . . . where?

In the duffel.

Right. Of course. In the duffel.

Behind their bifocals, Mr. Gold's eyes positively glittered. He cleared his throat, adjusted his scarlet bow tie, and resumed the story.

I'm sure you can understand my concern, detective, when I heard that there was a gun in one of our rooms. A handgun is not, after all, the type of item most hotel guests carry with them into an establishment like ours.

No. Of course not.

So yes, I did proceed to search the young man's room. As the general manager, I felt it behooved me to conduct an investigation.

And when you did that, when you *conducted your investigation*, did you find anything else besides the gun? Anything else that concerned you?

The manager's eyes crinkled with mischief. Clearly there was nothing he enjoyed more than this kind of amateur sleuthing.

Indeed I did, he responded, pausing for dramatic effect. A pair of binoculars, a map of Crooked River . . . And Colonel Mustard's candlestick, Kershaw thought irreverently.

And a receipt, Mr. Gold concluded.

A receipt?

From a motel. In Indiana. Specifically the Drury Inn.

Okayyyy. And this receipt concerned you . . . why?

Well, sir, I don't mean to sound presumptive, but doesn't it seem a little strange to you that a man traveling from New Mexico to the Florida Keys would stop first in Indiana? I don't know about *your* road atlas, detective, but according to *mine* that's a bit off track!

Excuse me, Henry, but how do you know he's traveling from New Mexico?

His license plate.

You checked that too.

I checked that too!

Despite his discomfort over the gun, at this point in the proceedings Kershaw was ready to dismiss Mr. Gold's suspicions about the guest in room 416 as one more example of the manager's feverish imagination. The hair dye was a dead end. Young people dyed their hair all the time these days. Sometimes purple. Sometimes orange. As for the surveillance angle, it sounded like braggadocio, a cocky young man with nothing to lose puffing himself up to a stranger. The receipt from the Drury Inn didn't raise any concerns either. Guy was on a road trip—so what? And finally, the binoculars sounded like another nonfactor. What better way for a young man to scope out the fair ladies of Crooked River as they shuffled back and forth across the central square? Only the Walther disturbed him, though not, in all honesty, unduly; a lot of people carried handguns these days, he reminded himself, and most of them were perfectly legal. No, there simply wasn't enough here to warrant any further action. He closed his notepad. He was ready to leave. It was Friday, he could knock off early, maybe do a little fishing before dark.

Thank you, Mr. Gold. As always I appreciate—

There's one more thing, detective.

He has a hole card, Kershaw thought. He always has a hole card. He glanced down at his wristwatch, envisioning the chartreuse jig skittering across the cove.

Speaking slowly, as if to make sure that he had the detective's full attention, Mr. Gold described Chance's admiration for William Dieter's novels. Matter of fact, he noted, the young man told me that the only reason he stopped in Crooked River in the first place was to check out the town he had read about in *Fever Tree*, maybe catch a glimpse of our reclusive writer while he was here.

Kershaw nodded, impatiently. Wondered where this was going. Wondered if it was going anywhere.

Well, sir, since he made it abundantly clear to me that he had never met our esteemed local author, you can imagine my surprise when I discovered a certain photo in his room.

A certain photo?

A certain photo that intrigued me so much I took the liberty to take a photo of it.

A photo. Of a photo.

Exactly!

And . . .

And I thought, the manager confided, reaching under the counter and retrieving a sealed envelope, that you might be interested in taking a look at it. So I made a second print, he said, handing Kershaw the envelope.

And now on his pontoon boat, as the wind dies down and the first faint stars blink on over the dusky water, Kershaw fingers open the envelope and considers the photo of the photo once again: Chance and William Dieter, a man Chance claimed to have never met, standing side by side. Smiling at the camera. On a beach in Quintana Roo.

dieter

At first, Faye wasn't able to recall with any kind of clarity what happened that day, wasn't able to reconstruct in orderly sequence or linear time her afternoon out at Lake Baylor, the evening meal she shared with Kershaw, or the drive back to town. But that doesn't surprise Dieter. Because that's how memory works, he could have told her, in bits and pieces, in fragments, in a burst of jazzy chords seemingly unconnected, arbitrary, stray.

At sunrise he writes, types, his desk facing the Indiana meadow where first light silvers patchy grass punctuated by the red splash of a trillium or a cluster of cobalt bluebells hanging upside down. Writes, revises, stops to eat breakfast, writes some more. Drinks so much coffee it's difficult to remain on task then switches to iced tea even though the tea packs a bigger wallop of caffeine than the coffee does. Coffee, tea, booze, the stress of facing, morning after morning, another blank page: it all adds up. What he should do is drink more water. But water's boring, water's tasteless, water doesn't kick him in the ass the way caffeine does.

The morning Faye drove out to Lake Baylor, high clouds drifted inland over aisles of fence posts on either side of the road while a black stream twisted across a pasture into the darkness of a tangled wood. As she headed east on Rutherford Road, the coastal landscape—horseshoe harbor and the dark waters of an estuary spilling across an open field—gave way to stretches of dry scrubland and occasional stands of sand laurel oaks. She remembers that at least. And then later, more, much more. Gradually it all comes back, the way childhood memories come back unbidden yet startlingly fresh. The serrated blades of palmettos glittering in the sun like the raised weapons of a standing army, a sea of bayonets. Swift clouds, a spotted pony in a paddock, a sun-faded barn. For a few more miles, the road meandered aimlessly, without direction, before eventually straightening out again. Crest of a hill then the road plunging down a sudden chute, an unexpected dip in the land Dieter sees in *his* mind's eye too, a heat-mirage of shimmering water at the foot of the pavement.

He hears Maggie rummaging around upstairs, clattering open a drawer to look for a pair of scissors or a ballpoint pen. It was so easy to shatter his concentration. Muffled footsteps on a carpet in a room two doors down unravels the next sentence. In the kitchen, Maggie whispers something to the boy and the thread of the narrative breaks. Like the clouds over the panhandle the writer's attention wanders, drifts. And yet omniscient, godlike, he still sees, if faintly now, whatever Faye sees. Fenced inland fields thick with mosquitoes and clotted with heat. A cloud of white dust as she turns off Rutherford Road onto a gravel track. Climbing out of Dieter's car, she notes a stillness she isn't used to, the air stagnant and unmoving without the breeze off the sea to shuffle it around.

Chitter of cicadas in the underbrush and the faint drone of a fighter jet high overhead. Then the first awkward moments in the foyer of Kershaw's house which smells, wonderfully, like rain, like old cedar barn boards stained by a flurry of rain. The detective shakes her hand casually, hoping to put her at ease before ushering her into the kitchen, a pleasant room filled with morning light and her first stirring view of Lake Baylor.

Dieter writes, types, eats a sparse lunch. Yanks the page out of the typewriter carriage and slashes a pencil across those unwieldly blocks of text, blacking out a word here, a word there, an entire paragraph.

Sometimes when Hunter hangs out with his friend Timmy Whitaker from across the road, Dieter and Maggie make love to rekindle the original flame, erotic heat followed by genuine affection, genuine tenderness, what they had when they started and somehow misplaced along the way. Because Maggie's unhappy, it's as simple as that. Even when Dieter's writing, even when he's deliriously lost in the story he's trying to tell, her unhappiness is there, a dead weight every word has to carry across the page. At times he catches himself staring without sight out the window, no longer lost in the story, just lost, and he knows that he has come to a crossroads and that his marriage is teetering on collapse.

Her first summers in Bloomington had been fine. She had her new garden to tend, volunteer work delivering hot lunches for Meals on Wheels, Hunter to entertain with games of Yahtzee or Risk. She attended a weekly yoga class, swam laps at the community pool, ate Indiana tomatoes right off the dewy vine. Like Jen she developed an easy, natural rapport with Dieter's father, skipping over to his house on Sunday evening with a slice of pecan pie. But when she came home, Dieter's relentless work habits left her stranded, isolated, alone. Even when he wasn't writing, he was writing, mentally constructing the next paragraph, the next sentence, the next word.

Thrown off balance by Maggie's severe mood swings, he promised to commit at least one day a week to trips around the state, just the three of them cruising down the scenic back roadways. On consecutive weekends they visited the limestone caves at Spring Mill, canoed the shallow waters of Sugar Creek, drove up to Parke County to tour the covered bridges. Hunter kept a journal, including photos he showed to Timmy Whitaker's parents when they invited him over for one of their belly-groaning dinners, meatloaf and mashed potatoes, something called succotash, a bowl of black-eyed peas. When she asks after Maggie, Hunter tells Mrs. Whitaker that his mother's fine even though he doesn't really believe it. Because Mom has gone quiet again, distant. Hunter pictures her standing on a dock watching a ship she wishes she had boarded sail away.

*

Kershaw unties the bowlines, turns over the engine, and steers the pontoon boat into the familiar channel. The wind is slight today, barely ruffling the water, the sun a torch. He hands Faye a bottle of sunscreen and returns to the wheel as she rubs the lotion on her arms, her shoulders, her legs.

Nearing the far side of the lake, he throttles back, allowing the boat to drift south. Then he props open one of the wells and retrieves a dripping shrimp bucket filled with shiners. He offers to bait Faye's hook but she smiles and says no, I'm good, I know how to do this. With a steady hand she spears the hook through the silver flesh below the dorsal fin, casts the shiner out toward the grass mats twenty feet away, and yanks the line at the last moment so it doesn't snag in the green tendrils. Time and again she casts the shiner along the perimeter of the mats the way her father taught her to fish in the shallows alongside the sunken logs in the strip pits south of Terre Haute or the deep green inlets of Paint Mill Lake.

On the fifth or sixth cast, she feels the first strike, a sudden thump that immediately tightens the line and drags the shiner under the mats. Instinctively she jerks the rod backward, securing the hook, the tension in her arms and wrists tightening the muscles and making them ache as Kershaw wheels the boat a few degrees west, helping her urge the fish back out into open water. From the arc of the rod he knows that whatever she's hooked is substantial, a striped bass or a channel catfish. Grinning his lopsided grin, he asks her if she's okay and she nods, gritting her teeth. Steady on, he says, I'm right here with you, I'll work the boat with you, and she hears a kind of reverence in his voice for the art of angling in grassy shallows and perhaps for her too, for her skill and patience, for her ability to land a large fish on her own.

Facing the meadow, Dieter taps the typewriter keys, falling under the spell of writing once again about Quintana Roo, fiction and memory joined, welded, forged. A bonfire on the beach, a gibbous moon rising over dark water. He types, remembers, relives it. The lisp of surf on quiet mornings when he went for a walk out to the lagoon before returning to core peppers or slice plantains in the restaurant of the hotel where divers from Madrid or Miami came for the reef, for the weed, for the hippie strays they seduced with romantic descriptions of shipwrecks off the coast of Spain. Parrish at sunrise sitting cross-legged in the sand watching the whitecaps roll in. Jen grilling pompano over fagots of native wood.

Coffee to sweat out last night's whiskey. A piece of dry toast to settle his indigestion. A page he will later, in a fit of pique, tear into shreds . . .

Afterwards she remembers how the wine Kershaw served with dinner loosened her tongue and how she began to talk about Mexico, about the village on the sea and the bonfires on the beach and the day Pablo Mestival showed up, tacking his sailboat into the lagoon. Afterwards, in wonder, even awe, she remembers how for the first time since the rescue she was able to describe to a stranger, as she hadn't been able to describe to her therapist or her parents or even her sister, Hannah, what really happened in Quintana Roo.

They ate on a screened lanai overlooking the dusk-shadowed lake. On the table, Kershaw placed two kerosene lamps alongside the brats he had just grilled and the potato salad he had made that morning. Famished, Faye forked a brat into one of the heated buns then sampled the potato salad, surprised by the unexpected sting of heat.

Tabasco?

No, chipotle, an old family recipe. Is it okay?

It's great, I like the heat. He showed her the chilled bottle of chardonnay, which turned out to be a lucky choice. Of course, she smiled, accepting a glass.

After a second helping of potato salad and a second glass of wine, she dropped her napkin on her empty plate. Then she looked him in the eye.

Dieter told you about me, right? What happened to me?

Yes.

She nodded, staring off through the black screen at the lake, the sky, the curved blade of a sickle moon slicing through the belly of a cloud. I don't mind you know.

No?

No. I mean you're a cop. You must hear, see, terrible things.

All the time. Comes with the job.

She nodded again, still staring through the screen.

Does it ever get to you, she asked in a small voice. The stuff you see?

Yes, it gets to me.

Do you dream about it?

I dream about it.

I see ghosts, she said. I see these ghosts.

He watched her carefully, trying to imagine how hard this must be for her to tell him these things. And how desperately she needed to.

Afterwards he held the half-empty bottle of chardonnay up to the kerosene light but Faye shook her head. Then how about coffee, he suggested.

Yes, let's have coffee. I need to sober up before I drive back.

Kershaw hesitated. He didn't want to sound too aggressive and scare her away, but if he didn't ask, he would always wonder what her answer might have been.

You could stay here, you know.

She lowered her eyes, staring down at the table, and Kershaw realized that he had made a mistake, a terrible miscalculation. After what she just told me, he chided himself, I suggest sex?

What I mean, he blurted out, is I have a spare bedroom. You could sleep there tonight and drive back in the morning.

Thanks, but I better get back.

Of course.

He walked her out to the car and opened the door. You sure you're all right to drive?

I'm fine.

Okay then. He offered his hand, casually, as he had when she first entered the house. But this time she held on to it with both of hers. Thank you, she whispered.

For what?

For taking me fishing. And for letting me get all that off my chest. All that baggage. All that . . . drama. Abruptly she let go of his hand and shook her head, looking off at the dark spaces between the trees. I just hope it wasn't too awful. I mean I hope you don't think . . .

What I think is you're a survivor, okay? What I think is you beat the odds down there by refusing to give up. What I think . . .(and here he hesitated, unsure how to go on, unsure how to say what he felt such a desperate urge to say) . . . Look, I'm just glad you didn't give up. 'Cause if you gave up you wouldn't be here tonight. With me.

He watched her bite her lower lip and he was afraid she was going to cry, something she hadn't done, not once, during her long and painful recital. Then he felt her hand cup the back of his neck and her lips press against his and when she finally pulled away, *her* grin was lopsided too. I've been wanting to do that, she murmured, all day.

While he caught his breath, she slid into the driver's seat and looked up at him. Will you call me tomorrow?

In lieu of a reply, he leaned down and kissed her through the open window, a gentle peck this time. Are you kidding? Of course I'll call you tomorrow. Whadya think this is, a one-time deal?

chance

On Sunday morning Chance followed Highway 98 north past the turnoff to St. George Island onto the bay bridge to Apalachicola, where traffic slowed for a tangle of cars arriving for services at the Episcopal Church. As he waited for the congestion to clear, he watched a procession of boats—shrimp trawlers, runabouts, oyster boats heading for the cuts beneath the bridge—troll out past the channel markers to the mouth of the river where the freshwater merged with the salt. Then the road opened up and he continued west across the peninsula, racing past long strands of sand until the traffic slowed again as he approached the paper mill at Port St. Joes.

A few miles east of Panama City he pulled into the parking lot of a convenience store to check the directions he scribbled down in his notebook the night before following his phone conversation with Señor. It had been a tough call to make, but who else could he turn to for help? That cop—at least he assumed he was a cop—sniffing around the Monte Carlo had thrown him for a loop. Pacing the floor of his room at the Gibson, he kept glancing out the window, wondering if Kershaw would return. With backup.

A dozen questions swirled through his mind. How did they make him? And why? He hadn't done anything since he arrived in Crooked River but walk around in a melancholy daze and hole up in his room. Why would anyone be suspicious? When his depression finally lifted, he had driven out to Christopher Key for a swim in the Gulf then treated himself to a couple beers and a plate of shrimp scampi at one of the dockside taverns. But he didn't talk to anyone at the tavern except his waiter. In fact, the only person he had spoken to at any length since he arrived in town was Mr. Gold.

Wait. Was it possible that Mr. Gold was the one who alerted the authorities? The nosy old manager seemed harmless enough, but his persistent questions, no matter how casually framed, might not have been as innocent as I assumed. And foolishly, I didn't shy away when he asked them. Why did I rattle on like that, talking about surveillance, my memoir, Dieter? The number one rule when you were on assignment was to play it close to the vest and keep your trap shut. And I didn't do that, I failed to do that.

Dismayed by his lapse in judgment, he had walked over to the Delta Café and ordered a burger and fries to go. Then hurried back to his room where he ate the burger, tossed away the greasy fries, and poured three fingers of Jim Beam into the single smudged glass the housekeeper had left on the bathroom counter. Sipping the whiskey, he looked out the window at the darkening plaza, two hippies chatting in front of Nirvana, a biker wearing his colors reeling out the door of the Blue Moon. He scanned the sports page of the local paper, searched in vain for something of interest on TV, and finally, for good measure, popped a Xanax before lying down.

Then at sunrise he woke with a blinding headache and a pervasive sense of dread. The cop would run the plates and find out that the name on the registration of the Monte Carlo didn't match up with the name of the guest at the hotel or the charge card he had used to secure his room. In other words, he was under suspicion. And nearly broke. Out of options, he had picked up the phone and dialed Mexico.

Unsurprisingly, Señor didn't sound pleased to hear from him. He listened without comment to Chance's report then advised him to sit tight, don't go anywhere, I'll call you right back. And three hours later, three impatient, antsy, nervous hours later, he finally did.

The Pelican Club, an elegant Spanish two-story perched on the crest of a sloped lawn above the grassy banks of St. Andrew's Bay, exuded privilege and wealth, with yachts of every size and stripe moored in the private marina and young black men with rakes and clippers tending the elaborate grounds, including the circular drive that swept past a row of cabbage palms to the club's imposing entrance, a pair of tall, intimidating mahogany doors. In front of the doors, a valet was waiting to park Chance's car.

On a side deck overlooking the tranquil waters of the bay, Harvey Bellum forked a mussel out of its shell and dipped it in a glass ramekin of melted butter. Catching sight of the maître d' escorting Chance to his table, he abruptly stood up. He was wearing an elaborate fishing vest with a maze of hidden pockets. Khaki slacks. Two-hundred-dollar sunglasses dangling by a cord.

Mr. Chance. He wiped his right hand on a napkin before offering it to his guest. Harvey Bellum. Please, have a seat. Something to eat? The food's excellent here.

Thanks but no, I'm good.

As Bellum withdrew his hand, Chance noted the gold Rolex, the same watch Pablo Mestival wore. Well how about something to drink then. Coffee? A cocktail?

A beer. A beer sounds fine.

Beer it is. Before sitting back down, Bellum lifted a finger in the direction of the bar and a minute later a waiter appeared.

Swallowing the top inch of foam in his glass, Chance studied Harvey Bellum. Mid-forties, fit as a fiddle, with a wave of salt and pepper hair falling, rakishly, an inch below his collar. Handsome. Well-tended. Unafraid. Chance guessed lawyer, one of many Mestival must keep on retainer for situations like this. Florida, he once heard, was a major player in the drug lord's ever expanding empire.

With an apologetic shrug Bellum held up his small fork. I hope you don't mind if I go ahead?

Of course not. Have at it.

Every year, Bellum said, chewing one mussel while stabbing another, I get a call from the chef here. The mussels are in, he tells me, the black mussels. It's all very . . . clandestine. No one seems to know where the mussels come from, or why they only appear once a year. A genuine mystery. He splashed the mollusk in the ramekin. Sort of like you, Mr. Chance.

Chance sipped his beer, projecting composure, professional calm. They didn't like it when you were in too big a hurry. Patience, a Shaolin virtue, was one of the rules of behavior you were expected to obey. Etiquette. Protocol. It was the emptiest kind of posturing, of course, but Chance didn't mind playing the game. Like James Bond, he was easily amused by the idiosyncrasies of his handlers.

With a contented sigh Bellum put down his fork, the dozen shells on his plate empty now. Took a sip of iced tea, carefully placed the glass on a coaster, and trained his gaze on his guest.

So I understand there have been . . . complications?

Yes.

Miss Lindstrom. She threw a wrench into the gears as it were, yes? By leaving Terre Haute?

Exactly. I wasn't expecting that.

Bellum wiped his lips on a napkin. Well I'm just glad, he proclaimed, we're *all* just glad that you were able to track her down to Crooked River.

Chance nodded, biding his time, waiting to see where this would go.

Unfortunately, Bellum added, I also understand that someone who may or may not be in law enforcement was seen taking photos of your car. Is that correct?

That's correct.

Do you have any idea why?

Not a clue.

Bellum smiled. Faintly. Enigmatically. Yes well, again, we're all pleased that you've handled this so professionally. It was wise of you to contact us before proceeding.

Bellum looked out at the bay where half a dozen small sailboats, Sunfish, skimmed the modest waves. In formation. A club of enthusiasts out on the water on a windy afternoon. So I suppose the only question at this point, he resumed, still watching the boats, is whether to go on.

May I speak frankly, sir?

Bellum swung his attention, his enigmatic smile, back to his guest. Why, of course you may. Please.

Chance glanced around the deck to make sure that no one was eavesdropping.

Look, if the guy's a cop, and I don't know that for sure, okay? But if he *is* a cop and he runs the plates on the Monte Carlo, it'll still be clean, right? Even if my name isn't the one on the registration?

Right.

Then I think we should proceed.

Bellum leaned back in his chair, a man at ease, in his element, on a Sunday afternoon.

Do you?

Yes I do. My record's spotless, Mr. Bellum, as I'm sure you know. They have nothing on me.

As far as you know.

As far as I know.

Out on the water the sailboats, in tandem, leaned away from the wind, like a nautical ballet, or a painting by Dupuy. Bellum drummed a finger on the table.

So what you're saying—and please correct me if I'm wrong—is that you still believe you can bring this, um, issue to a conclusion. A successful conclusion.

I do.

How long?

How long?

Do you expect it to take?

A few days, Chance answered.

On the outside?

A week.

Bellum paused to gaze out at the water again as one of the sailboats—a rogue—split away from the others, veering in a different direction. Then he shrugged, turning his palms up.

Would you excuse me, please? I have to make a call. Rising, he nodded at the empty mussel shells. You sure you don't want a plate of these? No? All right then, I'll be right back.

As Bellum crossed the dining room, Chance tracked him. At the bar, two middle-aged couples were sipping martinis. One of the women tossed her head back, laughing at something her companion had just said. Then her roving eye caught Chance's and she didn't turn away. They always look so cool, he thought, so pampered; and yet behind that beautiful façade they're just as lost, he supposed, as everyone else. Alcoholic. Sexually frustrated. Bored to tears.

Okay then! Bellum was back, flashing his moneyed smile. Looks like a go, he announced. Full speed ahead.

Great. So all I need now, Chance said—is this, Bellum interjected. He reached into one of his vest's hidden pockets and retrieved a white envelope. Everything you need is right here, he explained, tapping the envelope. Expenses. Directions to the car dealership where you'll do the exchange. And oh yeah, a brochure on the fish camp up on the Wakulla where you'll be staying now. You checked out of the Gibson this morning, right?

Right.

Then on your way back, stop at the camp and check in. They know us there.

Bellum offered his hand and Chance stood up to shake it.

It was a pleasure to meet you, young man. Take care of yourself. And good luck.

Chance stared at the envelope. It had all been decided, he realized, before he even left Crooked River. Bellum, Mestival's surrogate, had simply been testing his resolve.

Thank you, sir. I won't let you down.

Of course you won't! Bellum picked up his car keys from the table and slipped his sunglasses on.

By the way, I understand you're from Oregon. Eugene is it?

Yep. Eugene.

Beautiful country. I did some fishing out there once. Steelhead.

It was a great place to grow up.

I bet it was. And I understand your mother still lives there, right? In Eugene?

Chance hesitated before responding, his heartbeat suddenly increasing. There was more. Before they let you go, there was always more. Insinuation. Innuendo. A veiled threat. If you take off with the cash, if you get cold feet and don't complete the assignment, if you fuck up the deal, this is what will happen.

My mother?

Yeah, your mom. In that house on, what is it? Pershing Road?

Chance's mouth had gone dry. Without answering Bellum's question, he spun on his heel and marched away.

Beautiful woman, your mother, Bellum called after him.

He waited for the parking valet to bring the car, his swell of anger gradually subsiding. Looking out at the yachts in the marina, he vowed that one day he would board a ship of his own and sail into oblivion. Wake to the sun on the water and a brisk wind filling the sails as he parted the waves of earthly strife and passed, enlightened, through the "gateless gates" of satori.

On the highway he pressed down on the accelerator, rocketing past the slower traffic. After exchanging cars he would drive to the fish camp on the Wakulla and settle in for the night. And tomorrow, return to Crooked River. No more delays, no more second-guessing. He has known all along that it wasn't going to be easy to eliminate someone he once loved, but he has no choice now. He has run out of options. He has run out of time.

faye

Waking, fully rested, on Monday morning, Faye hears a stream of water sliding down the gutter spout then a clatter of fronds, the next-door neighbor's cabbage palm under assault as a thunderstorm off the Gulf sweeps across Crooked River. Wrapping the sheet and blanket tightly around her, she gazes out a window now streaked with drops of rain.

The rain will keep falling off and on all morning, but it won't dampen her spirits or temper her upbeat mood. For she has woken happy, miraculously happy. By telling Dave Kershaw about Mexico last night, a great burden has been lifted from her shoulders, and she feels light on her feet today, skipping down the stairs.

In the kitchen she looks out at the grey rain and leaden sky, considering the days, weeks, months she carried all those horrendous secrets bottled up inside her like a ticking bomb because she didn't trust anyone, anyone, to understand her plight. Not to sympathize but simply to recognize—clearly, without blinders—the evil the human monster she encountered in Quintana Roo embodies. All those interminable months she buried that knowledge, those primal emotions, those dreadful mental images so deep inside her no one, not her therapist or her parents or even her sister Hannah could possibly unearth them. On the other hand, if anyone *would* know how she felt it would be a cop. And that's what made Kershaw such a godsend. Without planning to, last night she had instinctively opened the bottle and poured the poison out, and no matter what happens between her and Kershaw now, she will always be grateful for his empathy. For his compassion. For telling her, when she finished, that she was brave.

As the latest shower passes over the neighborhood, followed by a brief lull in the storm, she takes Sunny for a quick jaunt around the neighborhood. By now many of the neighbors have gotten used to seeing her walking Dieter's dog and this morning one of them, an older gentleman standing behind the black mesh screen of his lanai with a book in his hand, waves. Smiling, she returns his greeting, still a little startled by her buoyant mood. Maintaining a firm grip on Sunny's leash, she pauses to admire the elegant old neighborhood, the trim green lawns and wooden sash windows, the flowering hibiscus and scarlet bougainvillea, the screened lanais where southern gentlemen nurse tumblers of Kentucky bourbon or read Shelby Foote's three-volume history of the Civil War. What a fine idea it was to come here. How—what was the word?—serendipitous? If she had stayed in Terre Haute she's convinced that she would still be miserable, still be paranoid, still be too fearful to venture out into the light of day. And her secrets would still be secret. But here in Crooked River she's free to ramble without worry through this charming historic neighborhood, smiling and waving at people she doesn't even know. When she first arrived at the village in Mexico, this was the attitude she projected. Optimism. Enthusiasm. Joie de vivre. And now somehow, after a long and tortuous interval, here was the joy of life again, tempered no doubt by what happened to her but not dead, not vanquished.

That afternoon Kershaw calls to ask about her plans for the rest of the day. She tells him she thought she'd clean the house, do a little grocery shopping, maybe stop by the nursery to pick up supplies for her next project, an herb garden this time.

So what would you think about meeting afterwards, around five.

Meeting?

For a drink, something to eat.

Are you asking me out on a date, sir?

I suppose, he says, I am.

She hears the amusement in his voice and realizes that they have already reached—built—a comfort zone, an emotional oasis where they're able to banter and flirt.

Well in that case, she answers, I accept.

Great. Any preference?

How about The Tides. Oysters and beer? I'm guessing a boy from Louisiana wouldn't object to a few fresh oysters.

On the half shell?

Of course. Is there any other way?

You have the *best* suggestions.

Oh yeah? Well wait'll you hear my other ones, she says, a little shocked by her audacity.

She hangs up the phone, tingling. Despite the horrific ordeal she had described to him the night before—a story that would have chased a weaker man away—Dave Kershaw is still clearly interested in her, as she is in him. Was this really happening? Like her newfound happiness, not that long ago the idea of a mature, healthy relationship with a man had seemed out of the question. Just as it now seems, against all odds, within reach.

chance

The fish camp on the Wakulla River wasn't much to look at, five or six no-frills rustic cabins, a rack of battered canoes for rent, and a prefab office with a pockmarked front counter and a cluttered, airless back room where the owner slept. Hardly the kind of place Harvey Bellum or any of his well-heeled associates would choose for a weekend outing, but it fit Chance to a T: off the beaten path, far from the nearest highway, and best of all discreet.

He rearranged the trunk of the Dodge Mirada—the car he had picked up the day before, per Bellum's instructions, in Panama City—placing the duffel back inside. Even though he planned to return to the fish camp that evening, if he happened to complete the assignment today, he would immediately head west, and he needed to have his belongings with him. Before closing the trunk he zipped open the duffel and removed the .380 and then, after confirming that the chambers were filled, locked the gun inside the glove compartment and started the car.

On his way to Crooked River, the sky abruptly darkened, and it began to rain so hard the windshield wipers couldn't keep up with the downpour, the lack of visibility finally forcing him to splash into the parking lot of an abandoned pizza parlor to wait out the storm. Ten minutes later, when the rain let up, he bumped back over a riprap of muddy ruts to the road.

As he drove into town, the rain started to pummel the hood of the Mirada again. Squinting through the windshield's furious wipers, he negotiated his way around the central square and eased over to the curb a block north of Dieter's house. Until this latest shower passed through he wouldn't be able to see much, but when it did clear, his vantage would be excellent, the view of the front door unobstructed.

Reclining the seat a few inches, he yanked his baseball cap low over his eyes and leaned back. He felt calmer today, safer and more secure now that he had ditched the Monte Carlo and checked out of the Gibson. He had to remain cautious, of course, but this was more his style, the kind of guerilla tactic Parrish used to describe when he and Chance, woozy from tequila, drank late into the night at the Yucatan Cafe. What you have to do, Parrish explained, is get in and get out. Obey your instincts. Make your move.

When the front door of Dieter's house swung open and Faye, looking much healthier than she had in Terre Haute, hopped down the steps and slid into Dieter's car, adrenaline surged through Chance's body as he thought about Parrish's words. Get in and get out. Limit your exposure. Do what you have to do.

Maintaining a safe distance, he tailed Faye as she drove out past the honey farms to a garden center south of town, where she piled a flat metal cart with half a dozen plastic bags of fill dirt and fertilizer and a cardboard box of fresh herbs.

Back at Dieter's, as Faye carried the garden supplies into the garage, he parked up the block again, a little paranoid now that the rain had stopped and people were working in their yards or chatting with a neighbor across a fence. Like the stakeout in Terre Haute, he was too exposed here, too vulnerable. But fortunately he didn't have to wait long for that to change. In a matter of minutes, Dieter's front door swung open again and a yellow Labrador pranced out, straining at her leash and dragging Faye across the lawn.

He would have to walk this time, and that was going to be tricky. On the other hand, now that the storm had swept through town and the sun glowed down on the sidewalks again, a number of residents were streaming back and forth across the plaza, providing cover. Sometimes it was easier to track your target through a crowd.

At the opposite end of the square, Faye turned west onto Banyan Street in the direction of the harbor. If he was lucky, she would veer south at the water and lead the dog to the small city park below the marina. Since that park lacked basic facilities—restrooms or picnic tables or grills—it was little used, and for a public space surprisingly private. The view to the east, toward town, was blocked by a tangle of Florida privet, to the north and south by black mangroves. An ideal spot, in other words, to complete his assignment. He patted the pocket of his jeans and felt the Walther pressing against the fabric and thought about the shadowy figure crouched behind the fence in the photograph in *Blow Up*. Clutching a gun.

He was itching to finish the job and move on. Freed of his debt to Mestival, he would be able to start over in Chicago or London or Rome. Crime lords were always on the lookout for good surveillance men, and with his track record in Mexico, he should be able to more or less name his price. Admittedly his final job for Mestival was particularly distasteful, but there was nothing he could do about that now. He had to put aside his petty emotions and complete the assignment with clarity and dispassion. Get in and get out, Parrish counseled. It was as simple as that.

Keeping the quarry in his field of vision, he passed through the working-class neighborhood where many of the deckhands lived. But when Faye got to the harbor she turned back to the north, toward the marina, dashing his hopes for a quick resolution. Apparently the gods were testing him again, measuring his Shaolin resolve.

When Faye disappeared inside The Tides, he looked around for a suitable spot to monitor the tavern. In the shadow of a crepe myrtle, in a ring of sodden red blossoms unloosed by the storm, he watched her step out the back door, still gripping the Lab's taut leash, and hesitate for a moment, scanning the cedar deck. Then she raised her right hand and Chance saw a man at one of the tables stand up and return her greeting and a cold bead of sweat—of fear—trickled down his neck and crawled underneath his collar.

It was him, the guy who had snapped the photos of the Monte Carlo. That firm jaw, slender physique, sideburns cut at a sharp angle below each ear: Chance would recognize him anywhere. Stunned, he watched Faye quickly cross the deck and lean in to kiss the man on the mouth while the yellow Lab, thumping its tail against the planks, waited impatiently for the cop to kneel down and pet her.

kershaw

Even though the rain had fallen in a fury, the tables and benches on the back deck of The Tides are already dry so they sit outside. Faye gazes up at the sky, momentarily transfixed by the remarkable azure bands, azure brushstrokes in the aftermath of the storm, radiating out from the axis of the sun.

It's so beautiful here, she says, the sunsets, the harbor, the boats. Do you ever take it for granted? You know, hardly even notice it anymore?

Kershaw raises his glass, savoring the cold sting of beer, and ponders her question.

Well I've been around water my entire life, he eventually replies, but no, I don't think I take it for granted.

It's part of you, who you are.

I suppose it is. He looks at the oyster impaled on the tines of her fork, which is suspended in midair, apparently forgotten.

So you gonna eat that or what?

Laughing, she swallows the oyster whole, chasing it with a gulp of wine.

She can't imagine a more pleasant spot for her second date with Dave Kershaw, her second date with anyone, it occurs to her, in the last four years. And yet even in the midst of their laughter and camaraderie she notices that Kershaw seems a little distant today. And that worries her. She fears that she may have been wrong about her confession, that all those graphic details might be causing him to have second thoughts about their relationship after all. Or perhaps there's another explanation for his apparent preoccupation, an unsolved case at the precinct or further complications as he attempts to repair, to re-establish, his relationship with his dad.

Listen, Dave, I get this feeling . . .

This feeling?

That something's bothering you. You seem a little, I don't know, pensive today?

He nods, unable to look her in the eye. Staring out at the harbor, he admits that there is, in fact, something they need to discuss.

Deflated, she puts down her fork and lifts the wineglass, her hand all of a sudden unsteady. Five minutes ago when she opened the back door and saw Kershaw waiting for her on the deck, her heart had pounded with joy. Now, blurred by worry, she watches him place a photograph on the table: two men standing side by side beneath a palm tree, smiling at the camera, a photograph she remembers taking one day on the beach behind the Yucatan Café. She can't comprehend why the photo is in Kershaw's possession, or what possible reason he has for showing it to her.

I know you know Dieter, he says, tapping the man on the left. But what about this guy?

She shakes her head, unwilling to accept what is happening. That morning, for the first time since she returned from Mexico, she had woken optimistic, genuinely optimistic. For once, the future had not seemed like a dead end.

Faye?

Closing her eyes, she sees the blue Monte Carlo race past Lureen's car a few days ago, traveling in the opposite direction, on the road to the beach on Christopher Key.

What kind of car?

A Monte Carlo. A blue Monte Carlo.

But you didn't say anything about it. You didn't tell me.

I didn't think it was important. I didn't think it was him.

Why?

His hair. It used to be blond.

Kershaw nods, checking another item off his mental list.

Chance, she mutters. It's like expelling a breath of bad air, poison air. He's *here*? He's really here?

Yes.

What the fuck?

When's the last time you saw him?

Four years ago. In the village.

Not since?

Not since.

It's unbearable, having to dredge it all up again. But what other choice does she have? She tells him about a conversation she overheard at the hacienda between a maid and the cook.

They were talking about Chance. They said he was working for Mestival.

Working.

They called him a contractor. I wasn't sure what that meant.

Sensing Faye's distress, Kershaw instinctively covers her hands with his own. Look, you're safe. That's the thing you need to remember. You're safe. Protected. You're gonna be okay.

You're gonna be okay. It was their mantra, their fucking mantra. Her mom and dad, Hannah. Her therapist. And now Kershaw. As if merely saying those useless words would somehow make them true.

Because she isn't okay, she's the opposite of okay. She's a target. Mestival has hired Chance—Chance!—to hunt her down because she knows too much, the location of his safe houses and airstrips, the names of his key associates. She glances at the photo again, recoiling, withdrawing. You were friends with him, Kershaw says. In the village.

Since this isn't a question, she doesn't feel the need to respond.

*

Dazed, she watches a woman in a red halter top trim the mainsail of a schooner named *Patti Belle*. Gaining speed, the boat hydroplanes across the harbor.

We ran the plates on the car, Kershaw says.

And?

And it's registered to someone called Herrera, Rafael Herrera. Name ring a bell?

No.

He registered it in Juarez. Recently. How about Juarez? You ever been to Juarez?

Not that I know of.

Kershaw pauses. He has to be careful not to offend her, not to push her over the edge.

I'm sorry, Faye, but what does that mean, not that I know of.

It means I went to all kinds of places, she snaps. Immediately embarrassed by her outburst, she lowers her eyes and takes a deep breath to control her anger, her frustration, her mounting fear.

They kept moving me around, she resumes in a calmer voice. Sometimes I didn't know *where* I was. Coulda been Juarez. Coulda been Tijuana.

I'm looking for the connections.

But you're off track, Dave. You gotta understand something. Mestival has people everywhere. *Everywhere*. And not just in Mexico either. Guatemala, Belize, Honduras. Right here.

Here, as in Florida?

Florida, California, New York.

You know this for a fact.

New Orleans. LA. Wherever.

She's lost her appetite but not her thirst. If she had her druthers, as her father used to say, she'd drink the heart right out of this perfectly awful afternoon. She feels Kershaw's eyes on her as she drains the glass of wine.

He's seen it before, every cop has. The glazed expression, flat affect, shock of disbelief giving way to despondency. Sometimes they checked out on you right before your eyes. I'm sorry, he tells the woman in the doorway, but your husband's dead, ma'am. Your daughter. Your boy. Going through the motions, because she doesn't know what else to do, the widow who refuses to admit that she's a widow invites you into her house for a cup of coffee. Or gently, very gently, shuts the door in your face.

The *Patti Belle* bounces back into her line of sight, powering through the chop, through the lemon light that floods the water and the azure bands that continue to lengthen, slicing through the crowns of the palm trees out on Christopher Key.

What a difference an hour or two makes. The elderly gentleman standing in the screened lanai who waved at her that morning was holding, in his other hand, a book by Shelby Foote. Or a tumbler of aged whiskey. When she returned his wave, did it a spark a moment of happiness, a sudden memory of the afternoon he strolled through an apple orchard in southern Indiana with the first girl he ever loved?

Faye?

She's smiling now, freefalling through that dark space that isn't quite shock but isn't quite not shock either. Limbo.

We need to talk about this, okay?

Fine. Talk.

In Mexico, in that village, did you and Chance ever, you know . . .

Have sex?

Yes.

No. He wanted to—believe me, he wanted to—but I didn't think of him in those terms.

But *he* did, right? Think of you in those terms?

Oh yeah. He was all in. Head over heels.

Since Kershaw hasn't touched his beer in the last five minutes, she picks up his glass and chugs it, then signals their waitress for another round.

Mindy?

Yeah, Mindy. Did he ever mention someone named Mindy?

She thinks about it for a minute. Then mutters, sarcastically, his first girlfriend. His famous first love.

When Faye excuses herself to go to the restroom, Kershaw pores over his notes, reviewing the day he just spent assembling a preliminary file on Albert Chance. Running the plates on the Monte Carlo and the credit card Chance used at the Gibson and discovering the discrepancies. Calling the detective out in Eugene. And finally talking with Dieter. At some point Patty Jones flounced into the precinct room, flopping down at the one desk she damn well knew he couldn't help seeing when he glanced out his office door. Spinning slowly in the chair until she faced him, her knees drifted apart. Flustered, he had picked up the phone again and dialed the Gibson.

That receipt you mentioned the other day, Henry, the one from the Drury Inn. You didn't happen to notice the town it was from did you?

Matter of fact I did. Let's see now. Oh yes, here it is. That property's in Terre Haute. On South Third Street.

Uh huh. South Third Street, Kershaw repeated, jotting it down.

Would you like a copy of it, detective?

A copy?

Of the receipt.

You made a copy of *that* too?

Dieter wasn't buying it. Forget it, Dave, he said over the phone. I mean he may—well okay, he *is*—apparently following her, maybe even stalking her. But sent down there to kill her? There's no way. He's the wrong man for the job.

Why?

Because Albert Chance is a phony, a fake. He used to follow the Vietnam vets around that village like a puppy, lapping up their words. Especially Parrish. And pretty soon he developed one of those classic delusions of grandeur, this harebrained idea that he'd turn himself into some kind of mystical warrior, a Shaolin warrior. Said he was gonna wander the desert for forty days and nights, like Jesus. I mean that's how he put it, okay? *Like Jesus.* Until he found The Way. That's Way with a capital W. He's a whack job, Dave, a loose wire. But a killer? I don't think so.

We have reason to believe that he's been working for Pablo Mestival.

As the seconds ticked away Kershaw waited, in no particular hurry, for Dieter's response.

In what capacity?

Surveillance. Tailing rivals, enemies. Taking photos. Setting up blackmails. That kind of thing.

Okay, I can see that. He *was* a camera buff, and work like that would feed his fantasies. He could imagine he was James Bond. But that's a long way from assassin, Dave. Besides, he was crazy about her, loony.

About Faye.

Yeah, Faye.

Kershaw consulted his notes.

He ever talk to you about someone named Mindy?

His girlfriend in Oregon? Yeah, sometimes.

Ever mention why they broke up?

He did. Apparently she was screwing around with other guys. With a *lot* of other guys.

Kershaw flipped to the next page in his notebook.

So there's this detective out in Eugene, okay? I just got off the phone with him. He thinks Chance killed her.

Killed who?

Mindy.

Another long pause, the weight of Dieter's silence again.

She's dead?

Fell off a cliff on the Oregon coast a few years ago. Hiking with you know who.

Kershaw can almost see the stunned expression on the writer's face.

Dieter? You still there?

Maybe I better come down.

No, that isn't necessary. We've got this under control.

When Faye returns from the restroom, Kershaw assures her that it's just a precaution.

But what about Dieter? What if he calls?

I already talked to him. This morning. I told him you and Sunny were gonna spend a few days out at the lake until this all blows over.

Blows over huh.

Listen, Faye, every cop in this town, and in a few neighboring ones too, are looking for that Monte Carlo. And sooner or later it'll turn up. I just think it's better for you to lay low until that happens.

While Faye packs, Kershaw walks out to the patio, remembering how Jack Maguire once told him that a cop can't afford to become emotionally involved in a case. You have to keep your distance, Maguire cautioned. Because if you don't, and it all goes wrong, you'll blame yourself for the rest of your life. Isn't that what happened to your dad?

I don't know, Kershaw answered. He doesn't talk about it.

Of course he doesn't. They never do.

Maguire was right, of course, but it was already too late for that kind of detachment. The players have assumed their positions. The plot, real or imagined, has been set in motion. The game is on.

maguire

Maguire looks terrible. Jowly, unshaven, the sleepless pouches under his eyes as dark as dried blood. While Kershaw fills him in on the details, the detective sergeant's gaze drifts over to the family photo on his desk, Mabel and the two boys on the Chris Craft. There's been talk of trouble at home.

Kershaw begins at the beginning, recounting how Dieter initially sketched in Faye Lindstrom's recent history—her confinement and eventual escape from Quintana Roo—before asking Kershaw if he would stop by the house and introduce himself when she got into town.

To put her mind at ease, Maguire says.

Right.

If she had any questions or concerns, she'd have someone to call. That kind of thing.

Exactly.

Fine. So you went to the house and introduced yourself.

No, we met by accident. In front of Nirvana.

Maguire doesn't reply. He looks bored, distracted, preoccupied. Beyond the closed door Kershaw hears a telephone ring in the precinct room and a muffled voice answer it. Sensing that he's losing his boss's attention, he skips ahead.

Cased the joint?

Kershaw shrugs, apologetically. *His* words, he says. Henry Gold's words. He likes old movies.

Maguire shakes his head in bemusement. The day he was promoted to detective sergeant no one was particularly surprised, or even remotely resentful. Least of all Kershaw, who still considers Jack Maguire a friend, a mentor, and the finest cop he has ever worked with. Lately, though, Maguire's marital issues have put a strain on their relationship. On a lot of Jack's relationships.

You got nothin', Dave.

Surprised and offended by Maguire's brazen reproach, Kershaw waits a few beats, determined not to lose his cool.

Nothin'? Really?

Less than nothin', Maguire insists, refusing to back down. Look, I'm not certain of the finer points of the law here, but I'm pretty sure Henry Gold stepped over some kind of legal line when he started casing, to use *his* word, that room.

Inadmissible. That's what you're sayin', right? Inadmissible?

That'd be *my* guess. If there was an actual case here, that is. Which there isn't. By the way, who gave you authority to put out an APB on that Monte Carlo?

Excuse me?

Maguire tilts his head back and looks up at the ceiling. Then he lifts a weary hand, conceding. Fine. Whatever. You wanna put out an APB, put out an APB. But I gotta tell ya, what you've given me so far doesn't amount to a hill of beans.

What about the gun, the .380?

Lots of folks carry guns, Dave. When you go on vacation, you carry a gun?

'Course I do. But I'm a cop.

Not when you're on vacation.

Kershaw hesitates, trying to regain his footing. So what about the photo then? Why would he lie about Dieter? Why would he claim he doesn't know him, never met him?

Maguire rubs his eyes, the weight of the world on his back. There was talk of trouble at home, Mabel hitting the bottle hard then slurring her way through certain social functions she was required, as the detective sergeant's spouse, to attend.

We can't bring a guy in just because he lied. Everyone lies. You know that.

That detective out in Oregon. Guy was adamant, Jack. Said there was no question in his mind that Albert Chance killed his girlfriend.

Then why didn't they charge him? Why'd they rule it an accident?

'Cause there was no evidence, and no eyewitnesses. They didn't have any choice.

Maguire glances up at the clock on the wall. Drums his fingers on the desk, impatient for Kershaw to leave. But Kershaw isn't finished.

Cops that interviewed him right after the incident? Including that detective I talked to? Said he didn't flinch. Not once.

So?

Gotta be a hard-ass to stay calm and collected like that right after your girlfriend tumbles off a fucking cliff.

Yeah well, there's no law against bein' a hard-ass. There was, we'd have to lock up half this town.

Spotting Betty through the office window, Maguire holds up his empty mug. According to the rumor mill, Maguire's marital woes went beyond his wife's drinking. Mabel and another man, other men. Seedy encounters in a cheap motel in Panama City. At one time their marriage had seemed rock solid, a template. What in the world, Kershaw wonders, went wrong?

What else you workin' on these days, Dave?

Jessie Smith.

The missing witness?

Yeah.

What else?

That 7-11 thing. And Tommy Bouchard.

Bouchard? The biker?

Right.

When Betty brings in his coffee, Maguire takes a sip and cringes, burning his tongue. Bouchard, he spits. What a derelict.

No argument here.

You know what I think? I think a couple of those Angels from Oakland take that guy out they'd be doin' us a favor. They'd be doin' the whole world a favor.

So what are we sayin', Jack? You want me to drop it?

What *we're* sayin', me, Maguire responds, mocking his Cajun protege, is that maybe you should take a couple days off. Hang out on that boat of yours. Do a little fishin'.

Kick back.

Exactly. Kick back with your lady friend out there. I'm sure she'd feel better if someone was with her.

I'm sure she would.

Maguire's gaze floats over to the family photo again. Better days, the boys still at home, Mabel happy. Then he turns back to Kershaw with a weak smile, signaling a truce.

Look, you keep your eye on Faye Lindstrom and I'll dig around a little bit on my end, all right? See what I can find. But I'm tellin' you, Dave, I gotta have something more substantial than what you've given me so far to commit any more resources to this.

Maguire's tired eyes follow Kershaw as he shuffles toward the door. Mr. Gold, he mutters darkly. The guy with the most, how should I put it, *active* imagination in town? This is your source, right? Oh excuse me, I forgot, you have two sources, Mr. Gold and our friend Dieter. A snoop who watches too many old movies and a guy that gets paid to make shit up.

Kershaw starts to respond but Maguire, switching his attention to an open file on his desk, waves an impatient hand, shooing away a fly.

Go catch some specks, you. I got work to do.

maggie

They drove into Bloomington to see a dark, artsy movie called *Shoot the Moon* because the film's screenwriter, Bo Goldman, Dieter claimed, was one of the few writers in Hollywood who knew what he was doing. Unsurprisingly the movie was indeed well written, for Maggie's taste too well written. A bleak, brutal meditation on the collapse of a marriage, it trained an unflinching camera on the wounds husbands and wives inflict on each other over time. The husband, played by Albert Finney, is a successful writer, and as Maggie sat in the dark watching the depressing images swim across the screen, she wondered why Dieter had chosen this, of all movies, to take her to. Was he trying to tell her something? Was that final devastating scene, when the writer, in anguish, calls out his wife's name, meant to represent Dieter's plea to her to help him mend their crippled marriage?

After the movie they went to Nick's English Hut, a campus institution, for a beer and a bite to eat. The booths were dark, the beer Belgian, the burgers grilled to perfection.

You can't make it up, Dieter said.

Can't make what up?

It's one of those things we used to say down there, you know? You can't make it up. Someone would start to juggle some tangerines or Dennis Hopper would stroll into the Yucatan Café and we'd all look at each other. And someone would say, you can't make it up.

Maggie severed a french fry with her front teeth. She had the impression that this seemingly random remark, like so many of the seemingly random narrative threads in Dieter's books, was leading somewhere specific. True to form, he told her about Kershaw's phone call.

Who's Chance?

Guy I used to know, we all used to know, down in Mexico.

And Dave Kershaw thinks he followed Faye to Crooked River?

Yep.

I see. So what about you? Is that what you think?

I don't know what I think. I haven't got a clue.

Maggie chewed another french fry, pensive now.

Was that true by the way?

Was what true?

That Dennis Hopper walked in? Just like that? I mean you're all sitting around that bar or cantina or whatever you call it down there and Dennis Hopper walks in?

What can I tell ya, Dieter said with a shrug. You can't make it up.

But of course you can, Maggie thought. And you do.

Years later, when she reads *Flamingo Lane*, she realizes that the evening they went to see *Shoot the Moon* was the evening Dieter's literary dream finally came true, the evening fiction and real life merged into one cohesive narrative pattern and the book he was working on more or less finished itself. The same evening, it turns out, that Chance, who had tailed Kershaw and Faye out to Lake Baylor and established that she was going to be staying, at least for the time being, at the cop's house, drove back out to the fish camp on the Wakulla River. He planned to spend one final night there, retrieve his belongings, and pick up the rifle Harvey Bellum, after a perfunctory phone call on a private line, had secured for him. Deer rifle, Bellum confirmed. 30-06. With a scope. That do the job?

The next morning Ellis, the guy who owned the fish camp, walked out to the Mirada as Chance was shoving his duffel into the trunk. Neither his appearance—stringy black hair, unkempt beard, dungarees stained with oil—nor his manner were reassuring. He told Chance to pull around back.

The room behind the front office was in shambles: newspapers scattered across the floor, ratty curtains hanging limp from a broken rod, surly pit bull lying in the shadows watching Chance's every move. Ellis reached under the bed and retrieved the deer rifle, which was wrapped in brown paper. He handed it to Chance and led him back outside.

You don't know me, he growled as Chance reopened the Mirada's trunk. Anything happens, you don't know me. Never seen me. Never stayed at this camp.

Dieter put down his burger and took a sip of beer.

The guy in the movie, he said, the writer?

Yeah?

Not exactly a flattering portrait.

Not exactly.

Vain, jealous, bitter.

Distracted, obsessive, self-centered, Maggie added, filling in the gaps. Unhappy.

Okay, okay, Dieter responded with an uneasy laugh. I get the picture.

Maggie tracked a handsome waiter gliding past them carrying a tray of beers. Uncertain, she thought. Arrogant. Moody. Is that really what most writers are like?

I guess we need to talk, Dieter said, breaking the silence.

Maggie twirled her pint, sloshing foam against the glass.

Sorry, but I don't think so.

Why not?

Because that's what the couple in the movie did, remember? Talked about it. Then talked about it some more. And look how *that* turned out.

Then what do you suggest?

What I suggest, she answered without hesitation, is that we think about our options.

When Dieter lowered his eyes, a needle stabbed her in the chest, a prick of pity.

I'm tryin', Maggie.

I know you are.

I'm tryin' real hard.

She cracked six eggs in a blue bowl. Whisked in half a cup of milk, salt and pepper, a sprinkle of Italian herbs. Added chopped onion, bell pepper, and mushrooms. Beyond the window, Dieter and the boy raised their scythes in the air and swished the blades down through the knee-high weeds gathering in loose piles around Hunter's tennis shoes, Dieter's boots.

After they finished their omelets, Maggie cleared the dishes and carried them to the sink. So I suppose you'll be going down there, she said, rinsing a plate. In her peripheral vision Hunter's head swiveled from one parent to the other. Always watchful. Always careful. Not prone, like his parents, to impulse.

Dieter raised his hands, as if in apology. Tonight.

Tonight?

I got a red eye.

One by one she placed the plates in their slots in the dishwasher. It wasn't like him not to consult with her before he booked a flight, but she wasn't particularly surprised. They had become as wary of each other as two wild animals sharing a cage, politely distant even when they occupied the same room.

Everything would happen, he mumbled, staring out the window.

What? What's that?

Maggie was watching him, Hunter was watching him.

Nothing, he muttered. Line from a book.

*

I don't know what to do, she told Lureen on the phone.

Dieter had already left for the airport and Hunter was watching a nature show on TV, animals on a grassy veldt tearing each other to pieces. She cradled the phone, looking out the bedroom window at the stars shining down on the hills.

Then don't do anything, Lureen said. You need to give it some time, honey.

It's like I'm not there anymore, you know? Like he's so wrapped up in his work I'm no longer there.

He's a writer, Maggie. That's what they do.

That's what they do?

They live inside their heads. They're not really out here with the rest of us. Lureen looked over at Charley propped up on the other side of the bed polishing off a bowl of cherry ice cream. Maybe what *her* marriage needed was what her sister's apparently already had, some distance. She switched the phone to her other shoulder. Sleep on it, she advised. Maybe it'll look better in the morning.

Yeah, maybe.

And call me back tomorrow. We need to talk about Faye Lindstrom. Is someone really after her?

I don't know.

Whadya mean you don't know? You talked to Dieter about it didn't you?

He doesn't know either. That's why he's flying down.

Lureen paused, clicking her emery board against a fingernail. Charley set the empty bowl on the nightstand.

So you want me to go over to the house? Stay with Faye until Dieter gets here?

Thanks, but Faye isn't there.

What are you talking about she isn't there? Where else would she be?

She's staying out at Dave Kershaw's place.

Another pause, longer this time.

Lureen . . . There was no mistaking the warning in Maggie's voice.

Dave Kershaw's place, huh.

Take it easy, sis.

Lureen looked over at Charley idly clicking the remote control.

Lemme tell ya somethin', honey, at this point I'd take it any way I could.

chance

He eases the Mirada into a driveway camouflaged by unkempt hedges. In true Shaolin fashion he has followed his warrior instincts and once again his Path has been revealed, the next step in the journey an unoccupied cabin on the banks of Lake Baylor featuring a direct view across the water to Detective Dave Kershaw's humble abode.

He enters the front door, the one he jimmied open the day before when he tailed Faye and Kershaw out to the cop's house and watched them go inside, Kershaw carrying Faye's suitcase. A quick inspection of the cabin across the lake (covered furniture, stripped beds) had confirmed that it was unoccupied, its absentee owner likely a snowbird who spent the scorching Florida summers in a cooler climate up north.

In the kitchen a gust of woodsy air fills his lungs and a sudden memory of the commune on the Powder River flashes through his mind, his dad teaching him how to fly-fish the river for trout. As the sun lipped over the ponderosa pines scattered along the opposite ridge, the old poseur flicked his wrist, waiting for the yellow fly to land, without a ripple, in the center of the stream, exactly where he had aimed it. Standing behind the boy, he showed him the subtleties of presentation—the arc of the right arm generating the twist of the wrist—explaining how you had to coax, not bully, your prey.

Now he sets a sack of groceries—Swiss cheese and a loaf of bread and a bottle of cheap red wine—down on the kitchen counter before going back out to the Mirada to retrieve the rifle and binoculars as well as the flashlight he purchased earlier that day at a hardware store.

Then he flips the kitchen switch to confirm that the electricity is off, a blessing in disguise: lights blazing on inside the cabin might alert a curious neighbor.

At the commune, his mother dredged the trout filets in corn meal then fried them in butter and oil. Afterwards, at sunset, they sat out on the back deck facing the river, his father reading a paperback copy of *Zen and the Art of Motorcycle Maintenance* while his mother sewed a patch, a miniature American flag, on the torn knee of the boy's blue jeans.

To the son, that first summer on the Powder River still represents, in memory, Eden before the fall. At night, drifting off to sleep, he anticipated what tomorrow might bring. A game of catch with Jimmy Kirk. A rainbow trout striking his jig. Another peaceful meal with his parents. No more rancor, no more angry threats, no more marital anguish. It was a new beginning for all three of them in one of the most beautiful places they had ever been. In the mornings, a scrim of mist lifted off the water and curled around the trunks of the cottonwoods. Then the sun peeked over the eastern ridge and the first beams slanting down through the ponderosa pines on the sagebrush hillside sparkled on the river too, the water so clear you could track the rainbows as they wiggled downstream to pause in the swirling eddies. And so another day in paradise would begin, a few neighbors joining his father for morning yoga, his mother blowing on the embers of last night's communal fire, Jimmy Kirk, baseball glove in hand, sprinting across the grass calling out Chance's name.

As the light begins to fade on Lake Baylor he passes through the kitchen into the living room. A sofa and a pair of matching upholstered armchairs draped with white sheets, end tables piled high with back issues of *Field & Stream*. A Navajo rug, painting of old Key West by Mario Sanchez, wooden rack with two fishing rods dangling from its hooks. Even with sheets covering the furniture, it's the kind of warm, inviting home he would be perfectly content to live in, a rustic space that would allow him to reimagine, to relive, his summer in Eden, in solitude this time. Unwrapping the rifle, he leans it against the back of the couch. Across the water, Kershaw's pontoon, cleated to the dock, rocks gently in the wake of a passing bass boat.

When a light blinks on in the back of Kershaw's house, Chance steps outside to investigate. Focusing the binoculars, he watches the detective decant a bottle of wine and place it in the center of a farm table on the screened lanai, then return a few minutes later with bowls and glasses.

He walks down the sloped lawn to the edge of the water, keeping the lanai in his line of sight. The air is slightly cooler now, a steady breeze whistling in the leaves of a nearby willow and rippling the dark surface of the lake. Above the opposite shoreline a crescent moon tops a grove of white cedars, shining down on the lanai where Faye smiles at Kershaw as he lights a kerosene lamp at either end of the table and pours them each a glass of wine.

Chance refocuses the binoculars, irritated by the romantic tableau, the wicks of the lamps flickering in their clear glass globes while Faye and Kershaw lean over their bowls of pasta before lifting their wine glasses in a toast. He fights off the urge to retch. Because that could, that should, have been him. Not the cop, him. In the village he gave Angelina every opportunity to return his affection. Flirted, bantered, listened to her stories, laughed at her quirky asides. Offered his hand when they strolled down the beach. Told her time and again how lovely she was. And for weeks, for a month, never made an inappropriate suggestion or tried to steal a single kiss. Ever the gentleman, he was determined to wait until he was sure that she was ready.

The night he finally made his move, breakers thundered in off the sea—a storm was brewing off Cozumel—and rolled high up the beach, the turbulent weather enhancing Chance's ardor. Lying next to her on a blanket in the sand, he reached out and slid his hand inside her dress and discovered the hard kernel of her nipple. Then his tongue searched her mouth, and when she timidly reciprocated he knew that her desire now echoed his own. He would bring her to climax right there on the sand, and from that moment on she would be his.

And then, without warning, she pushed his hand away and jumped to her feet, brushing the sand from her dress and shaking her head in rejection. Raising her voice so she could be heard over the gusty wind, she apologized, profusely. She just didn't think of him that way, she said. Their relationship was deeper than that.

Deeper?

Our friendship, she cried.

Now he seethes, torn to the bone by jealousy as he watches Faye and Kershaw finish their dinner, recalling in the throes of his despondency the path of broken shells like a necklace of crushed pearls he followed down the beach back to the Yucatan Café that evening, where he drowned his sorrow in a bottle of mescal.

After a desultory meal and a glass of vinegary wine, he beds down on the couch and sleeps intermittently, his dreams and daydreams inseparable, a single vision illuminated by the sun riding the crowns of firs and spruces as he ascends the trail to Cape Falcon with Mindy. Weaving through pitch-scented woods past occasional glimpses of the sea, he hears a boom of waves crashing against the rock walls at the foot of the cliffs. Wind whipping the trees. Screaming seagulls.

At the Yucatan Café the bartender poured another finger of mescal into his customer's glass, keeping his own counsel. Sometimes the gringos—especially the vets but this one too, the one they called Chance—plummeted into their dark place, their eyes going blank. The thousand-yard stare, one of them called it.

Sipping mescal and looking out at the stormy sea, Chance pictured Mindy approaching the crest of Cape Falcon, the only flat section of the trail, while he remained a few steps behind, his inner voice counseling patience, Bodhisattva calm. By the time they traversed the cape and started down the opposite face of the mountain he would quicken his pace and catch up with her. Meanwhile his father rotated his right arm and zipped his line over the Powder River, recoiling his fist just in time to drop the fly into a swirling eddy where the trout liked to rest. The boy studied his father's technique, memorizing it, until his eyes snapped open and darted out the window at the blade of a moon severing a cloud over Lake Baylor.

Sometimes when they made love he was startled by how tiny the bones in Mindy's shoulders were. In her pelvis, her wrists, her hips. Bird bones; a sparrow. It wouldn't take much, it occurred to him one day, to crush them in his hands. Approaching the crest of the cape, he picked up his pace, closing the distance between him and the slut who fucked anyone, everyone; all you had to do, apparently, was ask. *If she comes so easily / what must she be to other men?* It was the poets, his mother claimed, who understood the hidden rhythms of the world, the music the rest of us couldn't hear. Not the priests, not the politicians, not the tycoons; the poets. She quoted passages of Frost, Wallace Stevens, Sylvia Plath. Frost quaint and ironic, Stevens indecipherable, Plath an open wound. He reread the poems in *Ariel*, never having encountered such raw emotion in poetry before, never having known such poetry even existed. Plath's spider web mind. Her insistent voice. *Daddy*. Woozy, he finished the glass of mescal and staggered back to his room above the dive shop where he heard, through Dieter's closed door, a song by Fever Tree, that pastoral flute. He twisted the key in the lock, collapsed on his rumpled sheets, and passed out. As the sun broke over the Powder River, over Cape Falcon, over Lake Baylor, he assured himself that the scream he just heard wasn't Mindy. It was a gull.

dieter

After an unusually calm flight with only a mild shudder or two of turbulence, Dieter's plane touched down at the Tallahassee airport just before dawn. Still groggy from a lack of sleep, he joined the queue of exhausted passengers filing silently toward the tunnel, picked up his rental car, a red Ford Capri, outside the terminal, and drove south toward the coast, past a narrow bend of the Wakulla River, a water tower smeared with graffiti, the salt marshes at Alligator Point.

As first light broke across the furled masts of a pair of sailboats anchored off Carrabelle, he considered the strange twist of fate that had brought him back to Florida. How odd it was that Albert Chance, of all people, the least likely ghost from his past, had reappeared. First Faye. And now Chance. Apparently Faulkner was right: the past is never dead, it's not even past.

In the Yucatan, Chance and Dieter had discovered certain shared passions: the psychedelic music explosion in San Francisco, mangrove snapper grilled over mesquite, *In Cold Blood.* Not infrequently, at sunset, when Dieter got off work at the hotel restaurant, they matched shots of mescal at the Yucatan Cafe, fished the lagoon for black grouper, or watched Sam Peckinpah flicks on Dieter's Betamax. But even though the time they spent together was invariably pleasant, their friendship was bound by a strictly defined, if unspoken, parameter, a border they never crossed. The kind of open, intimate relationship Dieter had established with Angelina and Jen (and at times with Parrish) was impossible with Chance, who insisted on projecting a cooler-than-thou nonchalance, a Shaolin detachment from tenderness, pity, or regret.

For Dieter, the sights along this stretch of Highway 98 have always been enchanting, like panels in an art gallery, one remarkable composition after another. A lone kayak gliding across a mirror-like estuary. The sun striking a flight of egrets rising, in a sudden cloud, from the tangled maze of a black mangrove. Every swerve in the road a lush painting or stark photo, depending on the light. And yet today his appreciation of these familiar seascapes is tempered by his preoccupation with the latest chapter in Faye Lindstrom's bizarre saga.

He still can't fathom it. Pulling into town, within sight now of the familiar horseshoe harbor and the causeway to Christopher Key, he recalls, in detail, his conversation with Dave Kershaw, still uneasy, still unsure. For all he knows, the detective's pet theory—that Chance has traveled all the way from Mexico to Crooked River to do Faye harm—may be nothing more than idle speculation, an unfounded suspicion, a veteran cop's understandable paranoia. What if Chance stopped in Crooked River simply because it was on his way to wherever he was going? Isn't that, according to Kershaw, what he told Mr. Gold? That he was driving down to the Keys? Or what if, having read *Fever Tree*, he merely wanted to determine if the fictional town matched the real one. And yet why, in either of those scenarios, wouldn't he have called his old friend, his old *compadre* first, and let him know his plans? Surely he wouldn't have driven all that way and not stopped to see me. No, now that he reconsiders them, Kershaw's misgivings seem warranted. Whether they're accurate remains an unknown.

The house, inside and out, is as clean and orderly as it was when he left. The refrigerator full, the pantry stocked, the tomato plants in Faye's new box garden already flourishing inside bright metal spirals stabbed into the tidy bed. Impressed, he crosses the yard for a closer look. Then he phones Kershaw to let him know that he'll be driving out to the lake later that day. He took a redeye, he says, and needs to get some sleep first.

Listen, Dieter, I got a favor to ask. Could you come out tomorrow instead? We're just gonna hang out here for the rest of the day but I need to go into the office tomorrow morning and I don't wanna leave Faye alone.

Sure. No worries. Just tell me what time.

After taking a nap, he props open his journal on the patio table and scans his latest notes. Was Maggie right? By asking Faye to watch the house, has he stumbled upon his richest fictional vein yet? Will the rest of the new book, in Maggie's words, write itself? In defiant response to those critics who chided him for following up the success of his literary first novel with a genre piece, he decided to up the ante by bringing even more conventional suspense elements into *Fever Tree's* sequel, and now, miraculously, real life has seemingly handed him the plot twists he has been looking for ever since that decision was made.

On the flight to Tallahassee his thoughts kept drifting back to the bizarre events unfolding in Crooked River. Faye (and Sunny) holed up at Dave Kershaw's house on Lake Baylor. Kershaw's boss, Jack Maguire, pursuing his detective's questionable leads. And Chance, unpredictable Chance, lurking . . . where? Knowing that he's been made—why else would he have left the Gibson?—has the would-be assassin hightailed it back to Mexico? Or is he still in Crooked River, flying under the radar, looking for an opportunity to strike?

Invigorated by the narrative options available to him now, he scribbles additional notes, filling in the timeline and plugging the holes in the plot. And yet a few minutes later, when he looks out at the new tomato garden, his mood abruptly darkens. He pictures an industrious Faye cutting and hammering the two-by-sixes, spading fresh dirt into the bed, and planting the vines. Such a burst of energy seems to indicate that before Kershaw told her about Chance she must have been happy here, at peace with herself, perhaps for the first time since she fled Mexico. She must have considered Crooked River a fresh start, a second chance, an opportunity to rediscover the happiness Pablo Mestival so cruelly snatched away.

pete

That afternoon Dieter slipped on a pair of old sneakers and went for a walk, crossing the town plaza as the shadows of dusk began to lengthen along the axis of sidewalks. For diversion, he decided, he would stroll over to the marina and have a drink at The Tides. Where he would no doubt banter with Pete Minger, the comically vain bartender, who would ask, as he always did, whether Dieter had written him into his new book yet.

'Cause I'd make a heck of a character, writer man.

I know you would, Pete. And I'm workin' on it. Trust me, I'm workin' on it. But it isn't that easy. Dieter glanced out the plate glass windows of The Tides at the boats in the harbor rocking on their chains. The thing is, you're such a . . . such a *complex* character. It's hard to capture your essence.

The bartender grinned, fingering his goatee, pleased with Dieter's observation. You got *that* right. Women been trying to capture my essence for years!

A group of deckhands stormed into the bar and clapped Dieter on the back. They asked him how the new book was going and what he was doing in town. They weren't used to seeing him in the summer.

Dieter tried to formulate an appropriate response then realized that it didn't matter because the deckhands weren't really listening. They were on a bender. The spring fishing had been bountiful and their pockets were filled with cash.

Pete worked the crowd like the pro he was, pouring pitcher after pitcher of frothy beer. As the noise level rose, a crescendo of louder and louder voices, an elderly gentleman at the end of the bar sipping a glass of smoky bourbon quietly watched the revelers with a bemused expression, perhaps remembering his own raucous youth.

Dieter felt a large hand grip his shoulder as one of the deckhands leaned in close, practically shouting.

So what's the name of the new one, D?

The new one?

The new book!

Flamingo Lane.

The deckhand grabbed onto the bar to keep from swaying, his expression sober now. Right on, brah, he murmured reverentially, offering Dieter his solemn hand.

After the deckhands, in another hail of high fives and fist bumps, stormed back out, heading for the next tavern, Pete asked Dieter if he wanted to grab a bite to eat. His shift was almost over.

Thanks, Pete, but I gotta pass. I'm having dinner at home tonight.

But I thought you said Maggie was still up in Indiana.

She is. I'm having dinner with her sister.

Pete immediately took a step back, as if Dieter had just slapped him. Whoa there, writer man. Lureen? Are we talkin' Lureen here?

We're talkin' Lureen.

Hey, no disrespect to Charley and all but I gotta tell ya, that woman is hot.

And married.

Uh huh.

And an evangelical.

Uh huh.

And oh yeah, she's family, Dieter concluded with a flourish.

Exactly what I said, writer man, that woman is fucking hot!

*

Apparently hoping to loosen his tongue, Lureen tipped the bottle of Cabernet again, pouring Dieter a second glass. Then she pried open the to-go containers she had picked up at The Lucky Star. Sweet and sour chicken. Moo goo gai pan. So speaking of marriage, she said, even though they hadn't been.

Dieter looked dreamily across the yard at the new tomato garden. Can you believe she built that all by herself?

Built what?

The tomato garden!

Oh yeah, the tomato garden. Here, Dieter, have some of this moo goo whatever.

Don't mind if I do.

By the end of the third glass of Cabernet, he was finally ready to talk. Fine, he said, whatdya wanna know?

I wanna know what's goin' on between you and my sister, that's what. C'mon Dieter, she cried, flapping her manicured hands, give it to me.

Unsurprisingly, Lureen's spontaneous *give it to me* unleashed a torrent of feverish mental images that left Dieter the wordsmith at a momentary loss for words. Well whatever's goin' on, he eventually conceded, it's been goin' on for a while.

I know it has, honey. Lureen nodded sympathetically, as if this were old news. Then her chopsticks paused in midair and she looked momentarily discombobulated. Wait a minute, *what's* been goin' on for a while?

Pleasantly soused, Dieter didn't feel like elaborating. Buzz kill, isn't that what the kids called it these days?

You look lovely tonight, Lureen.

The comment made her tingle but she wasn't going to let on. She pointed her chopsticks at him.

Now you stop that, Dieter.

Know what a guy down at The Tides told me today?

I can't imagine.

That you're hot.

Lureen perked right up. She leaned forward, giving him a clearer view of her ample cleavage.

What guy?

Actually he said that you're *fucking* hot.

Dieter!

Hey, I don't make up the news, okay? I just report it.

What guy!?

Each one of the tomato spirals, he noted, was a different color. Orange. Blue. Yellow. Red. Like the swirls in that psychedelic poster he gave Angelina in Quintana Roo, Dylan's curly locks a riot of garish pigments.

Lureen cleared the dishes. Over her shoulder she told Dieter that she and Charley had hit a rough patch too. A couple years ago.

That dress you're wearing, Lureen. It's very becoming. What there is of it.

I told you to stop that, she responded with a laugh, hoping that he wouldn't.

I mean it doesn't leave a lot to the imagination, does it?

Refusing to turn around and look at him, Lureen kept her smile to herself. She rinsed and washed the dinner plates then wiggled back out to the patio where a now-contemplative Dieter was staring deep into his glass of wine. He looked up at her.

What kinda rough patch?

Oh you know, the usual.

No I don't know, actually. What's the usual?

You know, she said, drifting apart? Taking each other for granted?

So how'd you get over it? Pray? Ask for the Lord's guidance?

Dieter . . .

Sorry. But seriously, how *did* you get over it?

Lureen shrugged, lifting her shoulders to remind her brother-in-law, as if he needed reminding, that she wasn't wearing a bra.

By having more sex, silly!

Really?

Really.

With each other?

Dieter!

She picked up the empty wine bottle, wondering just how loaded he actually was. He liked to joke around whenever she came over but she had never seen him quite this openly flirtatious.

At the front door she offered, as usual, her cheek. Then froze in astonishment when Dieter pressed up against her, his lips mashing her own. Her first panicky thought was to pull away immediately, but those lips tasted awfully sweet, so she lingered.

You better get some sleep, honey, she whispered.

Wait a minute, Lureen.

I gotta go, sweetie. You get some sleep.

Outside she swallowed a gulp of air to steady herself, wondering why she didn't feel ashamed. Still tasting the faint whiff of wine on Dieter's breath, she tilted the rear-view mirror, noting with perverse satisfaction that the writer's awkward but intoxicating kiss—before she pulled away, he had even darted his tongue in—had smeared her lipstick.

kershaw

On Wednesday morning Kershaw climbs out of bed and takes a long shower, trying to clear his mind of distractions and focus his attention on the task at hand. Yesterday, as they were finishing lunch, Maguire had called.

We found the Monte Carlo.

Where?

In the back of a used car lot. In Panama City.

I see.

The detective looked over at Faye, who was pretending not to listen by staring out the window at the afternoon clouds gathering, blossoming, over Lake Baylor.

I'm bringing him in, Dave. Tomorrow.

Bringing who in?

Harry Crosby, the guy that owns the lot. And I want you to talk to him.

Fine. What time?

Ten. Look, I can send a patrol car out, Maguire offered in a softer voice. Someone to stay with her.

That's not necessary. Dieter'll be here.

A pause. Kershaw looked over at Faye again, who was watching a bass boat, in no particular hurry, putter across the channel.

The writer, Maguire said.

Yeah, the writer.

Great. I suppose he'll put us all in his next book. He'll call you Dave Kershaw. And I'll be that other guy, Jack Maguire.

Kershaw considered denying this then realized that the detective sergeant was probably right.

Faye is already up, already brewing a pot of coffee when Kershaw, fresh from his shower, ambles into the kitchen. He's surprised by how well rested and upbeat she looks. As someone who routinely encounters cowardice—hard-ass perps bawling in the back seat of a patrol car—he admires her courage, her tenacity, her stubborn refusal, in the face of fear, to cave in. She pecks his cheek and squeezes his shoulder and pours him a mug of coffee. Out the window, the lake's pewter water trembles in the morning mist.

So you have to go in early huh.

Actually not till Dieter gets here. Not till nine.

Good. While I make us some breakfast, we can talk.

Talk?

I wanna hear about New Orleans. What it was like to grow up in New Orleans.

As he waits for breakfast he describes the house he grew up in on the Bayou St. John, the freshly-ground boudin his mother used to fry on Sunday mornings, his first plate of beignets not at Café du Monde but at a little corner grocery in Faubourg Marigny.

Smiling, Faye sets his plate down. Two fried eggs, three strips of bacon, yeasty rolls slathered with butter and honey. He digs in. Talking about his mother's boudin has made him ravenous.

In the spring, he says between bites, when he was a teenager, he would catch the City Park streetcar to the French Quarter then stroll along the river listening to a gospel singer's stirring rendition of "Amazing Grace" or to one of the makeshift horn ensembles in Jackson Square. On Ursuline Avenue the ornate balconies were strung with colorful beads. On Toulouse Street a cop bantered with the driver of a delivery truck backed up to a small café with a tub of crawfish on ice a chef would then transform, evidently through some kind of culinary black magic, his mother claimed, into the city's best etouffee. Gumbo, jambalaya, etouffee, he practically chants, his gaze unfocused, his voice a curl of smoke.

Faye tells him that she went there once. When she was a kid.

Oh yeah? How old were you?

I don't know, eleven? Twelve?

And?

And I loved it! We stayed at this quaint old hotel in the Quarter and got up every morning and just walked around, gawking. She laughs, deprecatingly. Typical tourists, right?

Kershaw shook his head. The thing is, when I was a kid I loved the French Quarter just as much as the tourists did. The music, the food, the energy. I took pride in the fact that people came from all over the world to visit my town.

But sometimes nostalgia hurt, too. The stately old St. Louis Cathedral darkened by a canopy of clouds, the earthen levees along the Bayou St. John, Royal Street in the rain. In his mind, in his heart, it was all gone now, ancient history. Even the memories have begun to fade.

So what about you? What about Terre Haute?

Faye laughs at the question but he doesn't take offense. When was the last time he heard, in this somber, solitary kitchen, a woman's laughter?

What can I say? Compared to New Orleans, Terre Haute's pretty, I don't know, bland?

It's a factory town, right?

Factory town. Blue-collar town.

Conservative?

You have no idea.

Kershaw glances out the window at the opposite shoreline, momentarily distracted by a glimpse of a man striding, through the mist, across the lawn behind Vince Richardson's cabin. He's surprised. Vince usually doesn't return to the cabin until September.

All I knew for sure, Faye says, when I was growing up? Was that I was going to leave. As soon as I was able, I was going to leave.

Kershaw nods, still distracted. At the edge of Vince's property the man slips into the shadows of a grove of trees and disappears. Why would Vince come back so soon? He spent his summers up north, in Michigan. Place called Rifle Lake.

So you went to Mexico, he says flatly.

I went to Mexico, she answers, following his gaze out the window. I went to Mexico. And now I'm here.

He shows her the .45 he keeps in the top drawer of his dresser. Nodding, she picks up the pistol and immediately flips open the magazine to see if it's loaded. Pleased by her apparent familiarity with the weapon, Kershaw grins his crooked grin.

You shoot.

I shoot.

Excellent!

Faye studies him for a minute, amused.

You know you look very . . . I don't know. Relieved?

No, no, I just didn't want to alarm you. Didn't want you to think—

It's okay, Dave. She touches his arm. I understand.

It's a precaution, that's all.

Of course it is.

She follows him down the hallway. He's carrying a briefcase and he seems more relaxed now, more confident, ready for the day.

So who taught you how to shoot, your dad?

Faye smiles, coyly. You really wanna know?

I really wanna know.

How about I give you a clue.

Fine. I'm good with clues.

I figured as much. You being a detective and all.

In the kitchen she clears the table and loads the dishwasher while Kershaw shuffles through the papers in his briefcase, making sure he has everything he needs.

It was someone in Mexico, she says.

Kershaw nods, still scanning a document. Let me guess. Dieter.

Nope.

Parrish then, the vet.

Nope.

He locks the briefcase and lifts his palms. Sorry, darlin', but I think I need another clue.

Faye shakes her head, grinning. So is that what you tell your suspects, I need another clue?

Sometimes.

She closes the dishwasher and switches on the pre-rinse. Behind a boarded-up cantina on the outskirts of the village, Chance balanced an empty beer bottle on top of a post. Then he showed Faye how to grip her left hand around her right to steady the barrel of the pistol. How to press, not jerk, the trigger. She closed her right eye, squeezed the trigger, and watched the bottle explode.

Kershaw looks befuddled. You're kidding me, right? Tell me you're kidding me, you.

You can't make it up, she shrugs.

Killer, Chance whispered, leaning in close.

At the front door Faye assures him that it's okay to leave.

You sure?

Of course I'm sure. Dieter'll be here any minute. And you need to get to work.

She tilts her face up for a kiss. On the lips this time. Go on now, she repeats, shooing him out the door. Go catch the bad guy. Isn't that what they pay you to do?

chance

Chance goes to the house and re-emerges a minute later carrying the 30.06. Then he marches back across the lawn into the grove of trees that marks the boundary of Vince Richardson's property. Leaves and twigs crackle under the weight of his boots. Overhead, an osprey screeches, circling the misty lake.

He's looking for a branch to balance the rifle on. And soon finds it, the bough of a live oak, nearly horizontal and more or less chest high. Placing the barrel in the crook of the branch, he peers through the scope.

Perfect. Like a golfer, he flexes his knees, easing the tension in his legs, and peers through the scope again. His line of sight, his field of vision, could not be better. Through a tunnel in the trees in front of the oak, he has a clear view of Kershaw's house, his boat, his driveway. And yet the woods remain thick here; if a fisherman happens to motor by he won't be able to spot the man aiming a rifle across the lake.

In the crosshairs he watches Faye step into the kitchen and pour herself a mug of coffee. At the same time, panning to the left, he sees Kershaw's car pull out of the driveway onto the gravel track that leads back to Rutherford Road.

He can't believe his luck. For some reason the detective, Faye's knight in shining armor, has left her unprotected. Is this the opportunity he's been waiting for? If Kershaw's going into town to work, she'll be alone for hours. But why would he do that? Why, if he brought Faye to his house for protection, would he leave?

Then again, maybe Faye's staying at Kershaw's house not for protection but simply because she wants to. Maybe their affair has already reached the point where they can't bear not to sleep together. It's a disturbing notion, and it rankles him, adding fuel to the fire. You would hope, he thought, that someone who had survived the kind of sexual trauma Faye had been forced to endure in Mexico wouldn't be so eager to hop back into bed with a man. But that was women for you.

He straightens up, swallowing deep draughts of air and practicing his *pranayama* until the flutter in his heart moderates and his mind grows still. His breath calm now, his heart quiet, his soul centered, he bends to the scope.

It's your move, honey, he whispers. Your move.

kershaw

He pulls onto Rutherford Road, leaving Lake Baylor behind. The mist that blanketed the water and the woods earlier that morning has finally dissolved, and shafts of sunlight now pierce the tangled branches of the roadside trees. He slips on his sunglasses, presses the accelerator, and almost immediately has to slow down for a John Deere tractor whose driver, on the next straightaway, waves him around. A few minutes later, as he negotiates a sharp curve in the road without taking his foot off the gas, determined to get to the precinct on time, he sees a red Ford Capri rapidly approaching from the opposite direction. And as the Capri flashes past, he notes that the man behind the wheel is Dieter.

Harry Crosby is portly, florid, and like many people who find themselves against their will in a detective's office, antsy. His eyes dart back and forth across the nondescript room: institutional green walls, silent black telephone, file folder propped open next to Kershaw's stained mug. It's a bare, depressing, minimalist space, a cave. Harry would rather be outside on the lot in the sunlight flirting with a middle-aged divorcee haggling price on a '78 Datsun. Or trolling for cobia off St. Andrew's Bay. Anywhere but here.

To Kershaw, Harry Crosby's nervousness is the first indication that he probably has something to hide. He finishes scanning the notes in the file and looks up with a faint grin.

So this guy came to the lot, what, last Sunday?

Crosby isn't able to hold the detective's gaze, indication number two.

That's right. Sunday.

And you were working.

I was working.

Kershaw's smile grows wider now, more congenial. So you always work Sundays?

Not always but yeah, I usually do.

Kershaw consults his notes again, an idle finger tapping the folder. That's funny, he murmurs.

What is?

No, it's just that one of your salesmen told us you don't normally work on Sundays unless there's, in his words, *some kind of emergency.*

Crosby tries, with little success, to shrug it off. Well let me tell ya somethin', detective, in the used-car business there's a lot of emergencies!

Kershaw nods, that disarming grin never leaving his face. I'm sure there is, Mr. Crosby, I'm sure there is.

Kershaw asks him about the registration on the Monte Carlo, whether the driver happened to mention why he was trading it in, and if a mechanic inspected the car before the transaction was completed. Mentally checking off each question, Crosby replies that the title and registration were clean, the customer didn't say (and Harry didn't ask) why he was trading it in, and yes, a mechanic went over the engine.

And it was okay?

The usual wear and tear. Nothing out of the ordinary.

Kershaw studies the open file again, his finger crawling across the page until he finds what he's looking for.

So the deal was the Monte Carlo plus, what, six hundred for the Mirada?

Right. Six hundred.

And the customer paid cash.

Correct.

Without taking his eyes off his notes, the detective asks, in a casual tone, if Harry knows a guy named Harvey Bellum.

Who?

Harvey Bellum, Kershaw says, looking up from the file. He's a lawyer.

A lawyer.

Right. A lawyer. In Panama City.

The used-car salesman starts to chew his lower lip, indication number three. In contrast, the detective looks serene, at ease, almost complacent. They're playing high-stakes poker, the chips are on the table, and he's ready to call Crosby's bluff.

Name rings a bell, Crosby admits, but no, I can't place him.

Uh huh.

Kershaw pauses, drags the tension out, lets Crosby squirm.

How about Mestival? Ever hear of a guy named Pablo Mestival?

faye

Faye claps her hands and shouts, C'mon Sunny, c'mon girl! And in the blink of an eye the Lab whips past her out the kitchen door. On Lake Baylor, now that the mist has dissolved, the sun sparkles in the wake of a boat trolling the channel, headed for the grassy shallows along the opposite bank.

Tugging on her leash, Sunny drags Faye across the back lawn to the gravel track that circles the water. Where they bear left, following the road past houses with trim lawns, metal tool sheds, and truck gardens. Cedar decks with shiny black grills and vistas of open water. A spray of camellias in a tarnished copper pot. The houses tend toward modest, a retiree's winter fishing retreat or a working-class family's dream of raising their kids in the country. Jon boats with trolling motors or occasional pontoons like Kershaw's cleated to the docks. Stands of cypress and oak separating the properties.

She wraps the leash around her wrist to make sure that Sunny doesn't bolt and continues down the gravel lane, considering how pleasant it would be to live here. A pickup rattles past, slowing as the driver slings a hand out the window in greeting, because it's the kind of place where neighbors wave even if they don't know you, where men drive pickups and children lasso fishing lines into the shallows, where locals gather on weekends at the Drop On In Tavern out on Rutherford Road to eat oysters on the half shell, drink pitchers of ice cold beer, and swap gossip.

But she won't let herself fantasize. Even though she knows in her bones, because women's bones know such things, that Dave Kershaw is falling for her, and that she's falling for him too, she won't let herself fantasize. Her sexual anxiety has discouraged them from making love yet, but Kershaw's interest remains as bold and enticing as the Louisiana Hot Sauce he liberally sprinkles on his fried eggs. His attention, his male regard, is provocative. But it also frightens her. In Mexico she buried her romantic inclinations in a very deep grave, and she's not sure she's ready to unearth them just yet.

dieter

As he approaches a sharp curve on Rutherford Road, he catches sight of Kershaw's car traveling in the opposite direction and raises a hand just in time to acknowledge the detective's spontaneous greeting. He also notes that Faye isn't in the car and assumes that Kershaw must have decided to leave for work a few minutes early knowing that Dieter, who had called before he left the house, was on his way.

The prospect of spending a lazy day out on Lake Baylor with Faye pleases him. He doesn't consider himself a protector—he's never been able to protect anyone in his life, particularly Jen—but he does take pride in his loyalty, and if Faye feels safer with him around, then so be it. He'll do anything in his power to bolster her courage in this hour of need. Until the crisis ends—until, that is, Chance is brought in for questioning or it's determined that he's fled back to Mexico—he, or Kershaw, will remain by her side.

Crossing a bridge over the murky trickle of a stream, he hears a sudden thump under the car, followed by a loud pop, and the next thing he knows the Capri is skidding out of control, one of the back tires blown out and the front right already slipping off the pavement. He slams his foot on the brake pedal and jerks the steering wheel violently to the left, but this only makes matters worse. Spinning backwards, the Capri careens off the road and shudders to a stop in a grassy swale, the blown tire hissing like a snake in the sudden silence.

Fuck!

He slams the side of his fist against the steering wheel, his heart drumming against his ribs. Creaking open the door, he climbs out to inspect the damage.

Punctured, the back tire hangs limp off the wheel. And even though there's a spare in the trunk, the Capri, facing forward, facing upward toward the road, has come to rest half in and half out of the ditch, the ground too steep, too uneven to secure a jack. He curses again. Why now? Why did this have to happen now?

Too anxious to wait for someone to stop and assist him, he struggles up the embankment and starts to hike east toward the lake. Wincing from a sudden prick of pain, he raises a hand to his forehead and it comes away bloody. But that's the least of his concerns. He's not exactly sure how far he has to go, but he knows that Faye is waiting for him and that she's all alone and probably frightened. If he has to walk the entire way, then that's what he'll do.

After pounding the pavement for ten minutes, he hears a distant sound, a distant hum, and quickly wheels around. The sunlight flames against the pavement but when he squints his eyes, he's able to see through the heat haze a battered pickup painted in a coat of grey primer roaring toward him. Finally! He raises his arms and waves them over his head. The driver can let him off at the entrance to Lake Baylor or maybe even at Kershaw's front door, and he can call a tow truck from there. Then he notices that the truck isn't slowing down but appears, in fact, to be accelerating. In disbelief he watches it zoom past him, horn blaring as a sudden gust of wind in the pickup's violent wake nearly blows him off his feet. Standing on the shoulder of the road with his eyebrow dripping blood and the sun pounding down on the pavement, he has no other choice, no other option but to start walking again.

maguire

After escorting Harry Crosby off the premises, Kershaw taps twice on Maguire's open door.

Can I use your phone, Jack?

Leaning back in the new ergonomic chair that was delivered to his office yesterday, Maguire nods. Go right ahead, you.

Kershaw picks up the phone and dials his neighbor, Andy Smithson. He's lying, he says to Maguire out of the side of his mouth.

Who's lying?

Harry Crosby.

How do you know?

'Cause when I mentioned Pablo Mestival he flinched. More than flinched. Practically fell out of his chair. He's lying.

Before Maguire has a chance to respond, Kershaw lifts a finger for silence. Andy? Dave Kershaw here.

How ya doin', Dave?

I'm fine, Andy. But listen, I need a favor.

Anything, Dave. What's up?

I know this is gonna sound kinda strange, but I want you to drive over to Vince Richardson's place. Don't stop. Just drive by.

Drive by.

Yeah, drive by and see if there's a car in the driveway, okay? Then call me back.

He gave Andy the number and hung up. Maguire was staring at him.

Who's Vince Richardson?

Gotta go, Jack. I'll fill you in later.
That'd be nice.

Five minutes later, back in his office, he picks up line two. It's Andy Smithson.

There's a car there all right.

What kinda car?

A Dodge Mirada, it's a Dodge Mirada . . . Dave? You there, Dave?

faye

In the crosshairs of the rifle scope, Chance focuses in on his target. Concentrate, he tells himself. Breathe. He sets his feet, bends his knees, centers the shot, takes a deep *pranayama* breath . . . and abruptly straightens up, flexing his right shoulder to ease a sudden knot. He grits his teeth in disappointment, in frustration. He knows that he has to do this, that his future depends on it, that whatever other options he once entertained are now gone. But he can't pull off a head shot, it's too violent, too graphic, too messy even though what he's doing, he reminds himself, is not his fault, it's Angelina's.

As a steady breeze skitters across the lake, rattling the leaves of the trees, he leans over and presses his eye against the scope again and refocuses on Faye perched in the captain's chair of Kershaw's pontoon boat, casting a line into the cove. Then he tilts the barrel of the rifle down a fraction and slightly to the right, aiming at the heart. She won't know what hit her, she'll bleed out quickly, it's more humane this way. Clenching his jaw, he presses his finger against the trigger, at the same time closing his eyes.

A fish, something substantial, suddenly strikes Faye's line, jerking her forward, and an instant later the bullet slams into her shoulder, shattering her collarbone instead of her heart.

As the report of the shot echoes across the water, Chance opens his eyes. But Faye is no longer there, no longer visible, the impact of the bullet has flung her off the chair.

*

Lying on the deck of the boat she stares, through a blur, at the yellow Lab leaning over her, whimpering. Instinctively she tries to lift a hand to comfort the dog, but the pain is so sharp the hand refuses to obey. Rotating her head a couple of inches to the left, she shudders. The top of her shoulder is missing, a steady trickle of blood is streaming down her arm, and a piece of her broken collarbone, the end as sharp as a shiv, is pointing straight up in the air.

She loses consciousness for a few moments then snaps back awake. There's a spray pattern of blood on Sunny's fur too, and the poor thing's still whimpering, frantic now, circling her. It's okay, girl, she groans, it's all right. But of course she knows it isn't. She's been shot, Chance has shot her, and now he'll come and finish the job.

Yet for some reason she's unable to fathom, she isn't particularly afraid. Maybe she's too numb, too emotionally drained to care. Or maybe death, once feared, now seems a blessing, an end to the sorrow, to the grief, to Mexico. She closes her eyes again—all of a sudden, despite the searing pain, she's exhausted—and sees Dylan saunter across a stage and assume his place in the glow of a red spotlight. But wait, it can't be Dylan because she isn't at a concert, she's lying on the deck of Kershaw's pontoon boat, her left shoulder is missing, and she's waiting for her assassin, her executioner, to come finish the job.

Everyone she has ever loved gathers around her now. She's sure of that. Her mother's kiss on the cheek is cool and comforting, a simple declaration of love. Unsurprisingly, her father's expression is more stoic: it isn't fair, of course, but this is what happens to wayward daughters. Then Jennifer takes her hand and leads her down to the lagoon in Quintana Roo to watch the dive boat sail away.

Dieter's at the wheel, heading for the channel, and her mother's standing next to him waving goodbye. She cries out in anguish, but Dieter can't hear her, her mother can't hear her, no one can hear her. At the edge of the lagoon, she falls to her knees, overwhelmed by a sudden desire to sail out to the reef and plunge through the opal water, to freefall past the coral walls into paradise or oblivion, whichever comes first.

Now she's warm. Safe. Amniotic. Floating in the womb of fluid that protects the unborn and those about to be unborn again. In her dream the sun pours light down on the lake, on the boat, on the trees that shade the cove. Then she opens her eyes and sees Chance, pistol in hand, gazing down at her.

dieter

At the sound of the first gunshot, he panics, sprinting down the gravel track toward Kershaw's house. Overhead he hears the screech of an osprey and the echo of the gunshot reverberating in the lakeside trees.

But at the edge of the back lawn, at the sight of Chance pointing a pistol down at Faye, who is lying on the deck of Kershaw's boat, he freezes, mesmerized by the cinematic tableau: the pontoon rocking gently in the chop, the sunlight in the cedars, the gun in Chance's hand.

How many thoughts can occur in an instant? He hesitates at the edge of the lawn, not out of fear but wonder, a sense of unreality, shock, as if his fingers, his helpless fingers, are hovering over the keys of a typewriter, unsure how to describe what he sees.

Chance will fire the gun. Or he won't. Faye will die, or survive.

The lines blur. His life's a book; everyone's is. *Roman à clef.* Is he frightened? Has the sight of Chance's handgun pointing down at Faye crushed his will, his nerve? Is this his moment of cowardice, his moment of shame?

Faye will die, Chance will elude the authorities, and Maggie will eventually abandon him because he's an observer, a literary voyeur once removed from the world's incalculable grief, a writer no longer engaged by reality but by its surrogate, the fictional characters in a fictional town that looks a lot like the place she grew up in, Crooked River.

How many thoughts can occur in an instant?

He takes a step across the lawn, then another. Hears Chance tell Faye to close her eyes.

Now he's running, sprinting across the lawn. Wait!

What does courage look like?

Faye says *no*.

chance

Close your eyes.

No.

Please.

No, I'm not going to do that.

Her defiance is exhilarating. She wants to spit in his face. Grab his throat and strangle the air out of his lungs. Scream in his ear that her last act on earth is not going to be subservience.

He can't look, so he turns his head at the last moment, his finger trembling on the trigger. Then he sees Dieter running across the lawn and his brief hesitation, that second of indecision—What's Dieter doing here? He's supposed to be in Indiana—changes everything.

Gathering whatever strength and resolve is left in her, Faye raises her right hand, the one clutching Kershaw's .45, and squeezes off a shot.

faye

She hears sirens, Dieter's voice, the panting dog. Feels something—A rag? Dieter's shirt?—pressed against her missing shoulder. Dylan is gone and the stage is empty though the red spotlight remains on. The auditorium's empty too.

A voice again, but this time it isn't Dieter's. Voices, plural. *Careful, Tommy, watch your step, buddy. Careful now.* Arms like straps link and lift her from the deck, carry her off the boat, place her on a gurney.

When she stubs her toe on a tree root poking up through the broken sidewalk, Jen wraps an arm around her shoulder, says *Careful, honey, those roots are a bitch.* They're walking home from the Yucatan Café, back to their little house at the edge of the village. The moon is gold, glowing, monstrous. Harvest moon, isn't that what they call it back home? Something about the seasons, the cycle of the seasons. Harvest moon. Jaguar moon. Over and over the village by the sea, the boats trolling out to the reef, Mexico.

A wave of sadness, a wave of nausea, then unconsciousness. She pictures Jennifer on the bank of the lagoon and says to no one in particular, to whoever might be listening, beauty, meet death. Death, beauty.

She's borne through the air like a virgin carried aloft to a sacrificial altar to appease the furious gods. Except the altar is surrounded by vials, tourniquets, tubes. And it's moving. There's a woman she doesn't know on one side of her, Dieter on the other. Dieter's holding her hand and talking to her in a voice so soft she can barely make out the words. She twists the dial, raises the volume, and hears those first aching chords, that somber flute, and all of a sudden she remembers the name of the band, Fever Tree, and the name of the song Dieter played for her one night in the room above the dive shop, *Jokes Are for Sad People*.

Her father's stoic but that doesn't mean he doesn't love her. It's not the same thing, she tells Parrish. They pass the bottle, listen to the bonfire singe and sing. Vietnam, Parrish tells her, is where you learn, like the Navajo, to stop believing in linear time. They pass the bottle, the Thai stick, quarter the yellow pill. It's not the same thing, she insists, remembering her father's quiet love, his stoic love, his silent suffering. At the A&W he showed her and Hannah how to grip the plastic rifle, how to shoot the metal bear. When Hannah, unlike Faye a poor shot, missed, she stomped her feet, shouted I don't wanna play this anymore!

Shoot the gooks, Parrish mumbles. Kill 'em all. I don't wanna play this game anymore.

The dive boat shudders to a stop and someone tosses in the anchor. *Stay with me*, Dieter whispers. Nodding, she follows him into the water where they waver, like buoys, over the beautiful reef. Then dive.

A long white corridor, blazing lights, a sense of efficiency. A circle of men and women clothed in smocks like angels, or wraiths. As she plunges past coral walls, lavender fans, sea whips, a needle pierces her skin. Fish mouths open. Voices fade. When someone—Her mother? Dieter? Jen?—murmurs *Angelina*, she flinches. Shivers. Starts to cry.

epilogue

It's one of the Florida Keys, one of the shining links in that golden chain of islands extending south a hundred miles from the mainland even though Dieter, calmly composing the story, methodically tapping his typewriter, isn't going to tell you which one. There's a security risk involved, so he would rather you picture what it looks like generically. How the morning sun slants through the blinds of the bedroom in the back of the small house at the end of Flamingo Lane, waking the woman from a dreamless sleep. How at noon the light, harsh and unforgiving now, glares down on the water, on the tin roof of the woman's house, on the rickety dock her skiff is tethered to. And finally how at dusk the same light filters through a scrim of clouds on the western horizon before bursting into sunset flames.

In the mornings, in the front yard, sipping coffee at a picnic table strategically placed for maximum shade beneath a flowering poinciana, the woman watches the dive boat round the tip of the island. Seven days a week it sails out early and returns around noon, the divers slouching on the wooden benches, their flippers and masks lying at their feet, their scuba tanks and snorkels racked on a shelf behind the bridge. Sailing by, the young man who skippers the boat raises a hand and Faye waves back, acknowledging one of her tenuous connections to the world she's left behind.

Every few weeks Kershaw, or Dieter, flies down for a visit. The detective bears gifts, spontaneous gifts, a spray of yellow roses to brighten her kitchen table or a wind chime to hang from the poinciana now shedding its red petals in the rain. Straddling a chair in the rustic kitchen with the windows open to an afternoon shower dimpling the grass flats and drumming a jazzy rhythm on the metal roof, he watches her chop celery and onions to complement the other ingredients, the shrimp and sausage and yellowtail snapper steaming in the black iron pot. One of my new specialties, she tells him with a touch of pride, a Florida version of that jambalaya you grew up eating in New Orleans.

Dieter brings her books, a case of chardonnay, and blank journals. For weeks he's been urging her to write down the seafood recipes she's been perfecting, the stews and soups and grilled filets of black grouper she catches from the bow of her skiff, skimming solo across the grass flats at dawn. Casual and upbeat, he projects the lighthearted, bantering, almost careless persona he has always projected around friends. But when she asks about Maggie, his still-boyish face, in the soft glow of the kerosene lamps she has placed on the picnic table, droops.

It's a trial separation, he eventually concedes. Is that the right term?

You tell me.

The plan, he says, is for Maggie to remain in Indiana for the rest of the summer while I stay in Crooked River working on the new book.

And after that?

He shakes his head: who knows? His goal is to counter the understandable distress of Faye's forced exile with confidence and good cheer, but in the flickering light of the kerosene lanterns, he looks just as broken as her.

Twice so far the two middle-aged men in suits and ties have paid her official visits. Determinedly polite, they interview her out on the lanai. Perched on the edge of a chair and thumbing through a pocket notebook, the one in the blue tie asks her to repeat certain items of information she has already provided—the location of the safe house on Isla Mujeres or the names of Mestival's key associates in Belize—while the one in the red tie watches her carefully, smiling automatically whenever she glances his way.

Before they leave, she asks them if they know when she'll be allowed to see her family. Briskly collating his notes, clearly impatient to return to the mainland, Blue Tie assures her that the agency is working on the logistics of the reunion and that she will receive an answer soon.

She dreams about Chance and wakes in a sweat, listening to a palmetto bug snap against the bedroom screens.

To calm down, to stop obsessing about it, she forces herself to picture, instead, the young police patrolman and his family, his wife and two children, who live next door in the only other house on Flamingo Lane. To picture, through the screen of buttonwood trees that separates the two properties, his patrol car pulling into their drive.

At dawn, on the incoming tide, she sets out, the motor of her skiff coughing awake then purring as the boat reaches speed. Bands of milky light dividing the shallows. Wispy clouds. On a narrow crescent beach midway down the island, half a dozen sandpipers peck at the sand and marl, racing back up into the shade of a pair of sabal palms every time a large wave washes in. Farther south, an arched bridge spans the next pass, that channel of deceptive water.

Wearing sunglasses against the morning glare, she casts a jig again and again until she feels the strike, the sudden weight of a mangrove snapper she'll grill that evening over a bed of smoldering coals.

In bed one night she confesses to Kershaw that she can't shake the image of Chance, shot in the temple, collapsing on the ground.

He does what he can to comfort her, rubbing her back as if she were a child. It was him or you, he murmurs. You saved your own life by taking his. He doesn't say, *and he fucking well deserved it*, but she knows that's what he's thinking. She wonders if he'll ever forgive himself for leaving her alone that day.

Exhausted, Dieter stops typing. Looks out the window and notices the first shadows of dusk inching across the back lawn, Sunny asleep beneath the lemon tree, a dozen ripe tomatoes hanging, bloated with juice, from Faye's spindly vines. Tomorrow when he drives down to the Keys he'll bring her a box of the tomatoes, a sack of lemons, and that new collection of short stories by Alice Munro.

Miraculously the shoulder hurts less and less with each passing day and one afternoon, with the defiant resolve of an ex-junkie, she flings the remaining Percodan the doctor in Crooked River prescribed to her into the shallows at the end of the dock. The shoulder will never heal completely, and the skin graft is an ugly slash of a scar, but she likes to trace her fingers across the ridge the way Parrish used to rub his fingers across the shrapnel wounds in his left knee. Evidence, proof that she survived. Twice, survived.

Dieter buys her a camera, a new Minolta with a telescopic lens. He wants her to take photos of the dishes she's going to feature in the cookbook he's already talked to a publisher about. Photos of the grass flats too, he says, her boat, the sun setting over the channel where she catches the fish she uses in the recipes.

But I can't do that, she says.

Can't do what?

Publish a book.

Why not?

Her eyes narrow and her voice rises, unexpectedly adamant, unexpectedly fierce. Because Mestival will hear about it. And he'll track me down again. He'll find me again.

Then we'll use a pseudonym. You can be someone else.

She seems surprised by the suggestion, momentarily taken aback. Instead of a sneer, instead of another flash of anger, a faint, wistful smile now. Someone else, she murmurs. You know that's not a bad idea, Dieter.

It's not?

Ever since I got back from Mexico that's what I've wanted, right? To be someone else?

Dieter slides the camera across the table.

Well here's your chance.

It's one of the Florida Keys, one of the shining links in that golden chain of islands extending south a hundred miles from the mainland even though Dieter, calmly composing the story, methodically tapping his typewriter, isn't going to tell you which one. He'd rather you close your eyes and imagine how the moon rising over the salt flats lifts her spirits for a few moments as she stands on the end of the dock finishing, after supper, her glass of chardonnay.

At dusk she trolls back to the house, riding the tide, which has finally ebbed, riding the shallow current. And then she sees them standing in the front yard and she panics, certain that something has gone wrong. Roping the skiff to a piling, she forces herself to march, on tottering legs, down the length of the dock to the yard where the two men are waiting for her underneath the poinciana.

What?

What?

What are you doing here? Why are you both here?

Dieter looks over at Kershaw and shrugs. It isn't the welcome they envisioned.

Well we heard through the grapevine, Kershaw says in his laconic bayou voice, that a fabulous chef lives around here. And we were hoping she might cook us a meal.

She feels faint. They're softening the blow. They're trying to figure out how to tell me. They don't know how to tell me. Which means it must be something truly terrible, another assassin on her trail or someone, her mother or father or maybe even Hannah, suddenly dead. A massive coronary. A head-on collision like Jen's. A stroke. Why else would they have come down together? They had never done that before.

Look, she says, unable to prevent her voice from trembling, unable to camouflage her fear, I don't need to be coddled, okay? Not after what I've been through.

Dieter shrugs again.

Who's coddling?

Oh I see, she says. So you think, what? That this is one of your damn games, one of your literary games? Well it isn't. This is my life. This is my fucking life. Just tell me what's wrong. Just get it over with.

Dieter looks bewildered now; they both do.

Nothin's wrong, hon, Dieter says. We were bored. It's Friday. We thought we'd fly down and spend the weekend with you, that's all.

She shakes her head. She doesn't believe him. But what if he's telling the truth? What if their motive is that simple?

Nothin's wrong?

Nothin's wrong.

Are you sure?

Is the Pope Catholic?

Listen, darlin', Kershaw chimes in, you gonna offer us a beer or what? 'Cause I'm kinda thirsty here.

And then they're all around her, surrounding her. Rubbing her arms, patting her back. Her circle. Her lovely, lovely circle. Wiping her eyes, she follows them into the kitchen where Dieter, flinging open the refrigerator and grabbing three bottles of beer, says, without a trace of seriousness, *what* literary games? The hell you talkin' about, girl?

ACKNOWLEDGMENTS

For their help with general background and research, I would like to thank Jon Applegate, Michael Hannon, and Amitee Swanson.

For sharing her invaluable expertise on police procedures, I would also like to thank Micki Browning, former police captain and author of the crime novels *Adrift* (finalist for the Agatha Award for Best First Novel) and *Beached*.

And finally, a special shout-out, from the rooftops of Crooked River, to Jana Good and Kayla Church.

ABOUT THE AUTHOR

TIM APPLEGATE was born in Ft. Benning, Georgia and grew up in Terre Haute, Indiana. In 1978 he obtained a B.A. degree in journalism and literature from Indiana University.

Tim has lived in Boston, Sarasota, Florida, and for the last twenty-five years, on acreage in the foothills of the coast range of western Oregon. Tim is married and has two daughters. He grows wine grapes, remains an avid hiker, and travels extensively.

Tim's poetry, essays, and short fiction have appeared in *The Florida Review*, *The South Dakota Review*, *Lake Effect*, and *Rhino* among many other journals and anthologies. He is the author of the poetry collections *At the End of Day*, *Drydock (and other poems)*, and *Blueprints*. His first novel, *Fever Tree*, was published in 2016. *Flamingo Lane* is the second novel of the Yucatan Quartet.